CW00592110

A Matter Of Chance

Sheila Sonia Thompson: a biography

I was born in Muswell Hill, London under a piano (it didn't foretell a musical talent) on 26 September 1917, during a Graf Zeppelin raid. My mother had taken refuge there to escape any bombs that might have been aimed at her. I was the second of six children. My parents separated when I was six and were later divorced. As children we flitted from place to place and I spent a lot of my childhood in France so am (roughly) bilingual. The only education I remember was at a dame school in South Audley Street in London run by a Miss Woolf. I was a Conti Kid too, and remember appearing in *Peter Pan* at the Palladium, but I wanted to be a ballet dancer. Unfortunately for me, but not the Royal Ballet, I slipped a cartilage at fifteen and couldn't continue training. I then worked in the publicity department of General Film Distributors and started writing short stories, poems and articles. Only two articles were ever published.

Not subscribing to my older sister's philosophy that money is power I enrolled at the University of Geneva in Switzerland in 1938 thinking that knowledge might be.

The war intervened in 1939 and in 1940 I married a Canadian pilot. He was sent to Canada as an instructor after his first tour of operations and I, slightly pregnant, followed on a Dutch banana boat – 4,000 tons – soon afterwards. Two children later he was back in England, and in 1943 I followed.

After a year I wrote my first novel *Like a flower* because I was so horrified at the suffering of the bombed civilians. They didn't have the much-vaunted stress counselling in those days – and bloody little compensation for anyone. It was my way of screaming. Back in Canada after the war I produced two more children and wrote when I had time, which wasn't often. We lived in Peterborough, Ontario, and I had a weekly column in the *Peterborough Examiner*. We also cleared land and built (with our own hands, or rather Bill's hands and my advice and applause) a cottage on an Indian Reservation to live in through the long school summer holidays. Eventually we moved to Jamaica (my husband worked for Aviannca, the national Colombian airline, and we moved a lot). My marriage was a happy one. We worked hard at it. I was left a widow after thirty years of marriage.

My older sister, Pamela Kellino Mason, writes. My younger sister, Diana de Rosso, who was an opera singer, also writes, and now my eldest daughter, Roma Wheaton, has her first book on the shelves. Both she and Diana write non-fiction at the moment.

I live in a small warden-supervised council flat. Newly built, absolutely modern, wonderfully heated, very small, which is a blessing to me as I hate housework and never hoover until I am knee-deep in dust. My hobby is cooking. Other people scrub floors, clean silver or drink under stress, I cook. Luckily I have nine grandchildren prepared to eat – all but two living ten minutes away. I love the sea, sunshine, children and France, not necessarily in that order.

A Matter Of Chance

Sheila Sonia Thompson

First published by Ringpull Press in 1994

Ringpull Press Limited
Queensway House
London Road South
Poynton
Cheshire
SK12 1NJ

A CIP catalogue record for this book
is available from the British Library
ISBN 1 898051 06 2

Typeset in 11/13 Monophoto Ehrhardt
Filmset by Datix International Limited, Bungay, Suffolk
Printed in England by Clays Limited, St Ives plc

FOR 'LES GIRLS'

Rosemary
Pamela
Georgina
and
Leigh

I

Fifi had nursed her anger all day. Now she had worked up sufficient rage and courage to telephone. She had never felt quite like this before. It was completely out of character. She was the peacekeeper, the one who said "Let sleeping dogs lie", the one who turned the other cheek. Nevertheless, she dialled Janice Martin's number.

As soon as Janice answered, Fifi said, without preamble,

"I want a short, straight answer from you, Janice. A simple yes or no. Have you been sleeping with my husband?"

There was an audible gasp, then a slightly shaky voice almost whined,

"Is that why you haven't asked us over recently?"

Fifi slumped against the wall. Her worst suspicions confirmed. No immediate, indignant denial from Janice meant yes, she had.

"No, it isn't," Fifi said coldly, "But every time I have put you and Brian on the guest list, Ian has said no. This weekend we have people coming, whom I don't know, and I mentioned that I would feel more comfortable if you two were here, and Ian got that look on his face. The look he had when I had invited Nancy Spencer to dinner and he had already broken up with her. A fact that I, poor ignorant innocent, did not know. He looked like that this morning and, although I couldn't believe that you would . . ." Her voice broke momentarily, then she forged ahead, "But I had to ask. To hear a denial."

"It wasn't intentional, Fifi. Honestly," Janice began. Fifi gave a dry laugh. "No, really," Janice gushed on desperately, "I met him by chance in London, and it just happened. And then I couldn't stop. He's so handsome and persuasive. But it's over now."

"Not for me it isn't."

"Oh, I am so sorry, Fifi, and so guilty. Having you as a friend is so important to me. If you have to hate someone," Janice begged pathetically, "hate Marge Hatton. She was the one who replaced me, or that new American secretary of his, Laurance Dee, who holds sway now. But don't hate me, please, we've been friends for years."

"So I thought. Thanks very much, Janice," Fifi said with heavy sarcasm, putting down the receiver as Gladys, her cleaning lady, came into the hall.

"Now, don't tell me Mrs Martin has been upsetting you with bad news just when you're so busy," she said, buttoning up her coat. "I thought you looked peaky this morning, and now you look as if you've come over all queer. Would you like me to stay?"

"No. No. I'll be all right. Thank you for offering, Gladys. No one will arrive before seven so I'll take a cup of tea upstairs, and lie down for a bit."

"Well, if you're sure. Put lots of sugar in the tea and take a couple of aspirin. Phone me if you need me."

The door banged behind her. Fifi almost ran after her to bring her back. But would Gladys know what to do? She had been with them for years. She had helped to nurse the children through measles, broken legs and tonsillitis. She had dried Fifi's tears each term when the children went back to boarding school, but would Gladys know about infidelity? Habitual infidelity. Was Ian a male nymphomaniac?

"I don't know what to do!" Fifi cried aloud to the empty hall. "I always loved him so much. What do people do?"

In times of shock, her mind registered, try strong, sweet tea. She made herself a cup and went slowly up the stairs. Her knees felt weak and she had never felt so cold.

She put the cup down on her bedside table, switched on the electric blanket, slipped off her shoes and got under the duvet fully dressed. She brushed her hair back with a shaking hand and her skin felt cold and clammy.

It was unbelievable. Ian, whom she had trusted so fully, and Janice, her best friend? And this on-going string of attachments? Fifi had willingly forgiven the Nancy Spencer episode. As Ian had pointed out at the time, she had been very preoccupied with the three small children, and he had felt rather left out. He had solemnly promised that that was the first, and would be the last, time. His marriage was vitally important to him and he would never do anything to jeopardise it. She must believe him.

And, like a fool, she did. It had been during this re-birth of their marriage that he had persuaded her to move out of London to Buckinghamshire, close to Cheswick Manor, her father's estate. Normally there was a waiting list for years to get a house in the village, but the Earl had pulled strings for his only daughter and her family, and Bryony had become theirs very quickly.

Fifi had missed London, her friends, the concerts, the galleries, the bustle, but Ian loved everything about the house. He was boastful about living in such an exclusive locality, impressing business acquaintances with Fifi's family connections there. He enjoyed the fact that his sons were at Eton. It didn't matter to him whether they were happy or not, or that Fifi missed them so much. He boasted that his daughter was at Heathfield, though he knew that she had wanted to go to Hurst Lodge, where most of her friends went. Yet, all the time, he was playing the country squire, the family man in public, he had been having one affair after another. Apparently they never lasted long – and he never seemed tempted to leave her, but should she be grateful for that? She had never suspected. What sort of a wife did this make her? She had always accepted his explanations for his absences. She even packed his suitcase for him! She had known his job necessitated travel, that sometimes meetings ended late and he had to stay the night in town, but how much had been work and how much fun? What a fool he must have thought her, or did he think about her at all?

She had wanted to go back to work and, with the children all in the schools he had insisted on, there was no reason why she should not. A refresher course would have been necessary. She had only just qualified as a physiotherapist when she married, but Ian had been horrified, indignant. What would people think if his wife had to work? Arguing that she didn't care what people thought, and that it wasn't a case of have to, but want to work, hadn't moved him. He could be so crushing and sulky when he wanted to, so she had given in, as usual. Although there was nothing to keep her at home now, he wouldn't take her on business trips with him. He had vetoed it on the grounds that he would be working all the time, and would have the additional worry that she was lonely or bored. He had talked her out of everything, and what was she left with? The ghosts of Nancy Spencer, Janice Martin, Marge Hatton and Laurance Dee, and God only knew how many others.

Warm now, and with her anger spent, Fifi drifted towards sleep. Suddenly a chuckle burst from her lips as she wondered how many women fell asleep counting their husbands' mistresses instead of sheep.

2

Ian arrived home before Fifi had finished dressing. As usual he "hello"-ed from the front door.

From force of habit she called back, "Down in a minute," before wondering what she was going to say when she saw him.

"With clothes on, please!" Ian responded with jocularity. "Geoffrey came back with me."

There wasn't much she could say in front of a visitor and although normally Fifi would have considered it ill-mannered for a guest to arrive more than an hour early, in this instance she felt nothing but relief. She would have time to think this whole thing through. A part of her wanted to rush downstairs and accuse Ian, scream and yell at him, rend him with her nails, and another part just felt nauseated and wanted to walk away, never to have to see him again, to leave this house and all the nefarious dealings she now felt had gone on within its walls, and be free. God, she prayed, just get me through this weekend.

Wearing black silk trousers and a loose cream shirt, Fifi walked into the small lounge. Glimpses of the luxurious cream and turquoise drawing room were visible through the large wrought-iron gates situated between the bookcases.

"You remember Geoffrey Hatton?" Ian said affably.

"Of course." Fifi extended her hand.

She had remembered Geoffrey Hatton, but as a much younger man. In three years his hairline had receded, and the skin on his face and neck hung in loose folds. A much too stringent diet, Fifi decided, but said, "You're looking well."

She also remembered vaguely a Mrs Hatton.

"Didn't your wife come with you?" she asked innocently.

"Oh, Marge will be along. She is coming with Ross and Kelly, our Canadian contingent. Kelly is a high powered

5

business woman in her own right, and Marge wanted to see her office."

Fifi hardly heard the last bit. The penny had dropped. Marge Hatton, the woman who had followed in the footsteps of Janice Martin, was coming to stay. One of Ian's invited guests. She stared at him unbelievingly. Did he actually expect her to cook for, and wait on, one of his mistresses? Hadn't he any decency left?

Ian raised his eyebrows questioningly at her cold stare. What the hell was the matter with her? There was no time to ask, Geoffrey was already expressing surprise that Fifi had remembered his wife.

"What a wonderful memory you must have. You only met Marge once. She must have made a real impression."

"She certainly did," agreed Fifi. She remembered that they had two sons, the same ages as Camilla and Percy. Before she could enquire about them, Ian handed her a gin and tonic.

"Marge was his secretary," he hissed. "Don't muddle her with the first Mrs H."

"I won't," Fifi said aloud.

Ian glared at her as Geoffrey said, "What?"

"I said I don't know the other couple. Ian usually keeps me away from his business associates. I sometimes wonder why."

There was an uncomfortable silence. Geoffrey looked at Ian, hoping for a lead. Did the remark imply that Fifi knew of Ian's involvement with his secretary? Ian himself was puzzled. This behaviour was so unlike Fifi. He had always been able to rely on her to put guests at their ease, to pacify irate wives, and drunken husbands. She was the epitome of the perfect hostess, or always had been. This evening she was less agreeable, not in what she said, but how she said it. He was feeling pretty irritable himself. The last thing he had wanted was a weekend with Marge in his own home. The affair was over, why couldn't she accept that? He had been avoiding her for weeks, but when Geoffrey suggested the weekend as a welcoming gesture to the O'Neills, he couldn't very well refuse. He was sure that it was

6

Marge's idea but, once an idea was planted in Geoffrey's mind, he thought it was his own and would never budge from it. This was definitely not the weekend for Fifi to be difficult.

Though his eyes were as cold as two grey marbles, Ian shot her a winning smile with his mouth.

"It's because I don't like to share you, my sweet, and I like to keep my home a haven of peace, untarnished by business."

"Oh, I do agree with you," Geoffrey sighed, gazing out at the lilac trees tracing the outline of the lawn, the shadowy form of the ancient mulberry tree lunging drunkenly over the path. "Sometimes I wish Marge didn't know so much about the business."

"It gives you something to talk about," Ian said cheerfully, and then added with relief, "Here is Marge now, with Ross and Kelly. I hope Kelly isn't going to tell us how to run our company again."

Geoffrey laughed ruefully.

"She doesn't understand that we have an end product and her company doesn't."

Kelly, thought Fifi after she had met her, understood everything. She was smartly dressed, but almost devoid of make-up. She wore glasses of exactly the same pattern as her husband's, and low heeled court shoes. She was interested in the style of the house, the age of the village, why they didn't have storm windows, and what it cost to heat the house in winter. Ross listened to her questions, nodding agreement. They were obviously the questions he would have asked if she had not been there.

Marge, beautifully dressed, beautifully coiffed and manicured, sat quietly beside Geoffrey looking admiringly at the room until she managed to get the floor.

"Your house is lovely," she said to Fifi, who wanted no compliments from her. "We were thinking of moving to the country." Turning to Geoffrey, she said, "We should look for somewhere around here. It's a very picturesque village."

"Unfortunately there's a waiting list for houses, Several years long," crowed Ian.

"And how many years did you wait?" she asked, with something closely resembling a smirk.

"Our case was different. Fifi's father is Lord of the Manor. All prospective buyers have to go through him, and we all pay ground rent to him."

"Aha!" exclaimed Ross, "Now we are seeing British despotism in action."

"Yes, well, if he can do it for one, he can do it for another," said Marge. "You'll arrange it for us, won't you, Ian darling?" adding in honeyed tones, "For me, anyway."

"These things can't always be arranged, can they?"

Ian looked lamely at Fifi for support, but she managed not to meet his eyes.

Marge noticed.

"I'm sure you'll manage," Marge said, quite threateningly.

3

In the normal course of events, Fifi would have had everybody seated for dinner by half past eight, before the pre-dinner drinks had become dinner, but such an intriguing argument had arisen that she didn't want to interrupt it. It was undoubtedly leading to something very informative. As the alcohol moved from empty stomach to hot head, Marge began to bemoan the fact that Geoffrey was refusing to take her on the trip to Bermuda where he, Ian and Ross were flying on the Monday. It was the first time she had not accompanied him in twelve years.

"He's probably got some bimbo already lined up," Kelly suggested.

"That is exactly what I thought," nodded Marge.

Geoffrey, very flushed, and more than a little drunk, protested, speaking very carefully.

"It's a long journey, for a short visit. When I'm not at meetings I shall be relaxing on the golf course. Women are prohibited."

"Aren't you even taking secretaries?" Kelly asked sweetly.

"One. We are all sharing Ian's," Geoffrey responded gravely.

"Surely not the new American one?" Fifi asked brightly. "Not little Miss Dee? Well! Shock! Horror!"

Marge and Kelly laughed delightedly, making it obvious to Fifi that they both knew of Ian's involvement with his secretary. Inwardly she blushed with shame for her public humiliation, and his lack of discretion and courtesy towards her.

"You're not so dumb." Kelly gave her a slightly drunken shove.

Ignoring the conversation, and trying not to show his confusion, Ian looked pointedly at his watch.

"When are we eating?" he demanded.

"Whenever," Fifi answered flippantly. "This year, next year, sometime . . ." then, seeing the scowl on his face, continued, "I'll go and serve it now."

As she left the room she heard Kelly saying, "I'm taking my secretary to a meeting in Paris next week."

"Lucky girl," sighed Marge, thinking enviously of the days when she had been a secretary and gone off to glamorous places with her boss.

"It's not a girl," Kelly laughed. "I figured what's good for the goose is good for the gander."

"I wish you wouldn't talk like that," Ross complained, "even in fun."

"Who said it's in fun?"

Ian left the room and stalked into the kitchen.

"What's the matter with you tonight?" he demanded, "The dinner's late, all our guests are quarrelling, and you're not doing anything about it."

"I'm getting the dinner now, what more do you expect?"

"I expect you to put our guests at their ease."

"I don't find myself at ease entertaining one of your ex-mistresses."

It was a bulls-eye. There was no mistaking the genuine surprise and shock on Ian's face. He was, for once, speechless. Who, he wondered, had been talking to her? Had Marge been in touch with her secretly? Had Janice? That cute little girl at The Bull might have talked, and then it would have got back to Gladys. Damn them all, he thought. I suppose there will be tears tonight, but as long as it wasn't too noisy he could cope, and Fifi would be calmed down by tomorrow. He was very proud of his perfect marriage, and he didn't want anyone to think there was a crack in it.

The dinner, though late, was faultless, perfectly planned and prepared. They started with iced vodka, blini and lump roe, followed by salmon stuffed with rice and mushrooms. Then whole poussin glazed with rum, with new potatoes and a green salad, and finally violet ice cream in biscuit cups.

Unfortunately, the rowing continued throughout the meal. Marge, drunk, was determined to make Ian pay for ditching her for someone younger, and went into details of his "little fancies", as she called them, at various company meetings in the past. She made each episode sound hilarious, but named girls that Fifi had met, typists she had heard mentioned, and a travel agent she hadn't. She sat there in a daze, unable to swallow, having hot and cold flushes, offering food to the guests and hearing her life crumble around her. A couple of times Ian caught her eye and his glass and wiggled it by his lips to indicate that it was drink talking, but Fifi knew she was hearing the truth about her marriage for the first time.

In the quiet elegance of the drawing room the conversation was more muted. Fifi served the coffee in a sort of trance, and Ian poured lethal portions of liqueurs. Geoffrey fell asleep in his chair.

"How rude," Marge said disdainfully. "He has all tomorrow morning to sleep."

"He certainly hasn't. We're playing golf," Ian corrected her.

"Ross isn't playing golf," Kelly announced. "He's taking me to Windsor to see the castle. That was the deal. If I came on this weekend, and came to the dinner dance tomorrow night, he'd take me to Windsor."

Ross looked a little shamefaced.

"I'll take you in the afternoon," he promised.

"Didn't you want to come?" Fifi asked, surprised to find that other women were forced to do things they didn't want to do, but were bribed instead of being bullied.

"It's nothing personal. I just don't like sleeping in other people's houses. I didn't know what it would be like either. Still, I'm glad I came, I like you. But a deal's a deal, and Ross is taking me to Windsor tomorrow morning.

"No, no," Geoffrey woke suddenly. "We're playing golf. It's a foursome with Angus Knox."

Kelly stood up.

"Give me the car keys, Ross. I'm driving home."

"And anyway you can't drink and drive," Ross told her without moving, "and you have drunk, and then some."

Furious at the way the men all stuck together, Fifi said, "I have a very good idea. The men can take their golf clubs and go to their game, and we can take their gold credit cards and go to Windsor. We can do the castle, and watch the changing of the guard, and then go round the antique shops, the jewellery shops, the china shops and the art galleries. Then we'll have lunch, and do the matinee. You'll love the theatre there, Kelly, it's all red velvet and gold leaf paint, and . . ."

"But we'll be back to lunch," Ian interrupted.

"And we won't," said Fifi firmly, "so you'd better eat at the club, or The Bull."

At the mention of The Bull, Ian decided to shut up. He didn't want a row in front of his guests.

After the guests had gone to bed, Fifi started tidying up.

"Oh, leave all that for Gladys and come to bed," Ian said impatiently.

Looking at him, Fifi saw that his eyes were moist and glittering, a sure sign that he was in the mood for sex. No way, she thought, and said calmly, "Gladys doesn't get here till ten, and you'll want breakfast before that."

"Oh God, yes. We plan to be on the course before nine, when it gets crowded."

"Well then? It won't take long. You go on up."

The last thing she wanted was for him to stay and help her, and he was just as pleased to escape. Perhaps whatever had caused her bad mood had passed. She would come to bed when she had left things ready, and he would make love to her, and tomorrow everything would be back to normal. She would have forgiven and forgotten. Women were like that.

Fifi worked slowly from room to room. She needed to unwind. Finally she laid the table for breakfast hoping that Ian had fallen asleep. She wasn't really tired, having slept in the afternoon. She made herself a cup of tea and sat with the lounge window open listening to the rustle of the leaves, and smelling the peaceful scents of the country at night.

When she crept upstairs, Ian was in a deep sleep with the light still on. Quietly she got out her morning clothes, took an old t-shirt to sleep in and, with her toothbrush and hair brush, went into her daughter's empty bedroom. She stood there for a minute, hearing in her mind the children's clear young voices, seeing their clean fresh faces, aching for them and the safe happy times that had been, and then she remembered that, he was cheating on her even then.

Camilla's old alarm clock served to wake her, and she was up and dressed and taking hot tea to everyone at 7.30.

4

Fifi offered everything she could think of for breakfast. Kidneys, fried eggs and bacon, scrambled eggs, fried bread and tomatoes, even American pancakes from a mix, knowing that she would be in the kitchen filling orders all the while Ian was in the house. She couldn't face talking to him in case she lost her temper and made a scene in front of other people. Even looking at his smooth, sly face brought back all the lies he had fed her over the years.

Unaware of any undercurrent of bad feeling, Ian was accepting the guests' compliments for the lavish breakfast as if he were responsible for it.

Kelly was so anxious not to miss a minute at Windsor that she left the table before the others and sped upstairs for her jacket, shouting down to Ross.

"Don't forget, I want your card!"

"Use yours, and I'll pay you back," he suggested.

"Not a chance. I'll take yours."

"And don't either of you try that one," said Marge, quite belligerently. "Come on, hand over." She accepted Geoffrey's, saying, "You spend enough on your children, now it's my turn." Then she turned to Ian and held out her hand. "Ante-up. *You* owe it to your wife."

Ian gave her a look of pure hatred and, stalking round the table, gave his card to Fifi personally, saying quietly, "Don't run it into the ground."

"I never have – yet," she replied.

Surprisingly, Fifi found the company of both the women quite enjoyable. They were in festive mood, and the driving took her mind off her problems. Once in Windsor she found their enthusiasm contagious.

After the tour of the castle, Fifi and Kelly stood by the kerb to watch the band, with the Guards, march up the hill. Marge left them and slipped into Caley's department store, from which she emerged with a Chanel handbag and an assortment of silk scarves.

"They don't take cards," she announced with amazement. "I had to write a cheque. Geoffrey will have to pay me back. I shan't shop there again."

Round the corner in Peascod Street, they found a china shop. Kelly, it transpired, adored china. She proved this by buying five Royal Doulton figurines.

"Much cheaper here than in Canada," she told them.

Fifi wondered if Ross would agree when he saw the bill was over £600.

They passed a jewellery store where Marge bought a watch, and a necklace of cascading pearls and crystal, then wandered on down to see what was playing at the theatre. The billboards outside announced Tom Conti in *Otherwise Engaged*, and at the bottom a printed note said, "This play is not suitable for children".

"That's my sort of play," cried Marge. "While Geoffrey was married to Nicola he never bothered with the two boys. Now he's hardly allowed to see them, it's all he thinks about."

Fifi managed to bite back her automatic response that it served him right, and hurried into the box office to reserve seats for that afternoon.

Suggesting that they went over the bridge into Eton to see what that had to offer took them past a rather exclusive-looking boutique, and Kelly and Marge, their arms full of clothes, disappeared into the changing cubicles. Fifi didn't feel in the mood for buying clothes until she spied a red chiffon cocktail dress. The colour immediately lifted her spirits. It had long sleeves, a high neck, and was a transparent tunic over a straight, tight, low-cut slip. It was not the sort of thing that she had ever worn, and she hesitated before trying it on, but the enthusiastic reception she received when she came out to show it off persuaded her to buy it, though it was £345, a price she would never normally pay for a dress she might only wear a couple of times.

"What does it matter?" demanded Kelly, "It's not coming out of the housekeeping, is it? Think of it as a present from Ian."

Kelly was captivated with some antique jewellery in Eton, and both she and Marge made Fifi buy a necklace of garnet flowers, which she neither needed nor wanted, but bought when Marge said, "Buy it. It will make up for that gold and diamond bangle Ian bought for Anthea in New York."

Fifi cringed at the thought of Ian so blatantly parading his extra-marital women.

They lunched at a French restaurant overlooking the river. Stuffed with good food and wine, and loaded with parcels which they deposited in the car, they managed to get to the Theatre Royal on time.

As Fifi had hoped, they were late returning to Bryony and the men were standing around, dressed for the dinner dance and impatient.

"We thought you'd got lost," Ross greeted them rather sulkily.

"I expect they did," Ian remarked scornfully, "but there's no time to discuss it now. You girls have got exactly twenty minutes to get ready."

"If you're in such a hurry, go on without us," Marge said airily. "We'll come on in Fifi's car."

Furious that Marge should try and take over the arrangements, Ian snapped.

"You'll come with us or not at all."

The weekend, he decided, was rapidly disintegrating into a company convention wrangle – thanks to Marge – instead of the elegant, peaceful weekends at home that he was used to.

When Fifi appeared in the red dress, Ross whistled.

"You look absolutely splendid," Geoffrey admired.

"Doesn't she though," Ian agreed. "Come on, into the car."

Fifi and Ian left the house last and he gave her a very hard smack on the bottom which brought an involuntary gasp to her lips, a reaction that pleased him. She had practically ignored him since his arrival on Friday, and a playful smack might remind his guests that she was his wife, and remind her of his presence.

What it did remind her of was his attitude that she was his possession, that he could do what he liked but she must follow the pattern. Steadying her voice, she said, "Marge and Geoffrey can go with you. I'll go with Kelly and Ross to show them the way."

It was such a plausible suggestion that even he could not argue with it.

Once at the dinner dance, Fifi had no trouble avoiding him. She had known most of the people there since childhood, these were her friends, though, she wondered bitterly, how many had been like Janice, betraying her for years? Nevertheless she allowed herself to be whirled off to dance or chat, pretending a gaiety she did not feel.

"Your wife is a very popular gal," Ross remarked as he, Kelly, Marge, Geoffrey and Ian found themselves once more sitting without her at their table.

Ian frowned. He had been waiting for a chance to dance with Fifi. He had never seen her in red before. He wanted to tell her it was her colour. She looked ravishing, so vivacious, really sexy. He felt like pushing her other partners away and telling them that she was his.

"Why wouldn't she be?" asked Kelly. "She's kind, and she's beautiful. And behaves like a real lady."

"That's just what she is, a real lady," Geoffrey told her. "Lady Florence Bannerss. Lucky old Ian."

Ian beamed. Glory, even reflected, enhanced his feelings of being a success. The top of the pile, he thought to himself happily. The man with it all! He couldn't understand the change in Fifi during the last twenty-four hours. He watched her flit from friend to friend. That, too, was unusual behaviour for her. Normally she sat with her guests and just nodded to passing acquaintances and friends. No doubt it was Marge's belligerent presence. He didn't like it himself. How he had ever got himself embroiled he couldn't fathom; she had been no easy conquest, hard to mount and even harder to dismount.

Back at the house they wearily made for their rooms, all except Fifi.

"Come on up," urged Ian, making no attempt to hide his eagerness. "There are no dishes tonight so we can indulge in a little passion."

A wave of cold anger swept over Fifi.

"I have no intention of sharing a bed with your penis, Ian. I don't know where it has been."

He recoiled as if she had slapped him.

"What the hell do you mean by that?"

She gave a loud sigh.

"I mean it's over. I'm through. You can sleep with whoever you fancy, as long as it's not me. I had intended to wait until everybody had gone home before I told you but, since you've asked, I'm telling you now."

"So, what changed since last night?" he leered. "You slept with me then."

"No, I didn't. If you imagine I did you must have had a wet dream. I slept in Camilla's room, which is where I'll sleep tonight."

"Well, that's a charming way to treat your husband. What will our guests think?"

"*Your* guests, and I don't give a damn what anyone thinks. What did they think about your bed-hopping on all your trips and overnight 'business' stays in London?"

Her voice was rising and Ian cast a nervous glance towards the stairs. Could they be overheard? Was anyone still awake? He had a reputation to consider. He was completely sober now and realised that some serious thought would have to be given to the situation to bring about a reconciliation and preserve his life-style. A wave of self-pity welled up inside him. He didn't want to lose Fifi. What was she thinking of? Perhaps she was going into the menopause; he would have to be patient.

"Keep your voice down," he warned. "We'll talk about it tomorrow when we're not so tired."

He turned rapidly and went upstairs. He would send her some lilies from Bermuda, and buy her something beautiful at the 'n Pond shop. He wouldn't sleep with Laurance while he was there, either. An act of contrition. Then he smiled at his own stupidity. How silly! Fifi would never know anyway.

5

The shrill twittering of birds woke Fifi at dawn on Sunday. It seemed to her that she had only been in bed for a few minutes, but obviously the night had passed, and in sleep. She made a mental note that the starlings were nesting again in the eaves above Camilla's window, and something should be done about it. Then she suddenly thought, "Do I care?" In that moment, her future plans crystallised. She would leave Bryony as soon as Ian went to Bermuda. She would go to London and start proceedings for a divorce. She was amazed at how painless this decision was. Cradled in the warmth of Camilla's duvet, listening to the increasing and ever more varied bird song, the whole idea seemed very straightforward and sensible. She got up and dressed slowly in a blue chambray dress from her summer wardrobe, which she stored in Camilla's room these days, and went out into the pale sun that filtered into the garden. Then, in a sort of daze, she made herself a cup of tea, mixed the eggs, milk, water and flour for her Yorkshire pudding to give it plenty of time to expand, and prepared the vegetables for lunch. She measured the coffee and water into her coffee maker. All her gestures were automatic, she was just repeating the Sunday pattern of years, her mind surprisingly, painlessly blank.

Suddenly, Fifi decided to go to church; God deserved some thanks for this feeling of peace that had descended on her. She was just about to slip quietly out the front door when a hand touched her shoulder. She jumped in alarm, but it was only Ross.

"Sorry about creeping up on you like that. Kelly and I didn't think anybody else would be up, so we crept downstairs. We wondered where the nearest church was."

"Oh!" Fifi couldn't hide her surprise.

20

Most of Ian's guests were of the new Thatcherite variety, more interested in banks and mints than churches.

"I'm going to the eight o'clock service myself now," she said. "But there is a family service at eleven if you'd prefer it."

"No, we'd much rather go with you, if you don't mind," Kelly chipped in.

"It's Church of England."

"That's near enough Protestant, isn't it?" Ross asked.

"Yes, I suppose so, but with a name like O'Neill, I thought . . ."

"I know. People always jump to conclusions," Ross interrupted her, and gave one of his rare smiles. "People think 'Irish', 'crazy Catholics!' My folks were Orangemen."

"It's so stupid really, sorting everybody into sects. Carrying on feuds from generation to generation," sighed Fifi. "For no reason either. We're all just people."

"Didn't your kids fight over nothing when they were little?"

Fifi nodded, smiling at the memories.

"That's all it is, you see," said Ross. "Half the world just never grows up."

They picked their way through an overgrown path at the side of the church. Kelly and Ross stood back to admire the stained glass window above them.

"That's my family tree," Fifi told them proudly. "It's a memorial window for someone killed in the first Great War."

"The church is pretty old, I guess," commented Kelly.

"My parents were married here," Fifi was amazed to hear herself say, "and I was baptised here."

Why should they want to know that, Fifi wondered. What funny ideas were coming off the top of her mind and getting out through her mouth.

"And you got married here," interjected Ross.

"That too," agreed Fifi, with a sigh.

"That's real continuity," Ross said admiringly, but to her receding back.

"Belt up, Ross. I don't think she wants to discuss that right now," Kelly told him, her feminine intuition on override.

21

In the dim, cool interior of the church, Fifi tried to thank God, but forgot what for. I'm losing my mind, she thought in panic, I don't know who I am any more. The familiarity of the hymns and the sermon had a soothing effect, and Fifi had to force herself to get up when the service was over.

She introduced the O'Neills to the vicar as they left and he said gravely, and with ill-concealed surprise, that it was a pleasure to welcome any of Fifi's guests, but if they had waited and come to the later service he could have offered them coffee.

Fifi hurriedly dragged them away.

"You don't know what you've been spared. I've had some of his coffee. Thank you for coming with me this morning."

"No favours. We go every Sunday, wherever we are," Kelly told her. "It helps us to keep our sense of values."

"You must have a wonderful sense of discipline," Fifi answered.

"We intend to survive the rat race, and come out as real people," Ross said. Fifi let them in the back door and they were welcomed by the smell of coffee. Hearing their voices, Ian and Geoffrey came into the kitchen.

"Where have you been?" demanded Ian, "We're champing at the bit for breakfast, and . . ."

"It's all laid in the dining room and will be ready in a minute. There's the coffee." Fifi pointed to the machine, feeling neither angry nor surprised at his apparent inability to pour a cup of coffee, a feat he had accomplished many times before.

"We've all been to church," Kelly announced. "You should have come. It helps to start the week right."

"I'm afraid God wouldn't recognise me," Geoffrey remarked. "It's so long since Ive been to church. Fifi, would you mind going up to Marge? She's in a terrible way. She's being sick, and crying. I don't know what's the matter with her."

"Hungover is the matter," Ian stated laconically.

"No, it's more than that. Would you mind, Fifi, seeing what you can do?" he begged.

Ian held his breath. After her outburst the previous night he was terrified of what she might say, but she gave her most charming smile and said, "I don't mind at all. I'll just get your sausages and mushrooms on the table and then I'll take her up some tea. Luckily we have a very nice doctor available, if she needs him."

Relief flooded Ian. Perhaps last night had just been a little aberration, being hurried to get ready, and then drinking too much.

Fifi herself was finding it difficult to understand how she could be feeling so calm and normal after the rage and anguish of the previous two days. The only trouble was that she felt calm but couldn't keep her thoughts together.

She found Marge propped up in bed, her eyes red with weeping, her face devoid of make-up and the skin pallid, her hair like a bird's nest. When the outside packaging is off we all look the same, Fifi thought, without malice or pleasure.

"Oh, Fifi. I feel so awful having you wait on me. I'm so sorry I've been sick."

"Well, you can't help it. Have you taken Eno's or anything to settle your stomach?"

"Nothing is going to settle this. Oh God, Fifi, I don't know what I'm going to do. 'Sick in the morning, pregnancy dawning', they say." And she burst into tears.

"The sickness doesn't last forever,' Fifi comforted her, "and pregnancy isn't the end of the world."

"It is for me," wept Marge. "Geoffrey hasn't been able to get it up for months, and . . ."

". . . and he's hardly going to buy an immaculate conception?"

"Exactly. So what am I going to do?"

Fifi could not suppress a little tingle of pleasure as she said,

"Why don't you ask the other man concerned?"

"He doesn't want to know. He's ditched me for someone else. Nobody lasts more than two minutes with him."

The situation began to strike Fifi as funny, and a little tragic.

23

"Don't you think that asking your lover's wife what to do about his bastard is a little OTT?"

Marge sniffled into a wad of Kleenex.

"I was afraid you knew. Actually, I came down intending to tell you, but you've been so nice, so polite and kind – it doesn't make me like myself very much."

"I've come to the conclusion that it takes two to tango, so I don't blame you particularly. I'll give you my advice – for what it's worth, considering the pathetic mess my own marriage has been. You'd better pretend you've got a 'flu bug now. Tell Geoffrey that you'll spend a couple of days in bed and, as soon as he's gone in the morning, rush to your doctor. He might give you the morning-after pill, but, if it's too late for that, have a D and C. If he won't do it, try the Marie Stopes Clinic. But don't waste any time. And don't move out of bed till he's gone tomorrow. It's when you move that you throw up, and two days running might make him suspicious. After all, Nicola had children, so he must know some of the symptoms."

"Thank you, Fifi, you've been a brick. Ian doesn't deserve you."

"No. So next time you choose someone else's husband make sure that he's someone who is thoughtful of his wife, then he'll be thoughtful of you."

"But Ian is thoughtful of you. You're on a pedestal. You're his madonna, the rest of the female race are all whores." Marge spoke bitterly.

A sudden enormous pain shot through Fifi, a real physical pain as if all the other women who had shared Ian were stabbing her at the same time. She rushed from the room so that she didn't cry out in front of Marge.

Training from infancy in good manners, to be polite and thoughtful, to do and say the right thing at the right time, helped Fifi to get through the day. At 4.15 Ross packed everybody into his car, with the luggage and the accumulated treasures from the shopping expedition. He refused tea on behalf of all of them, insisting that he had to get ready for

Bermuda, and that Geoffrey wanted to get Marge to bed. Mindful of Fifi's advice, Marge was complaining of shivers one minute, and hot flushes the next.

"Sounds more like the change of life and 'flu to me," Ian cracked, muttering under his breath, "and I couldn't wish it on a more suitable person."

As the car drove away, Ian tried to put his arm round Fifi's shoulders, so that their guests' last view would be of the perfect couple waving them goodbye, but Fifi managed to duck inside the front door and he had to follow her.

"I think that went off very well," he announced, sinking back into his chair and draining the remains of the cognac from his balloon glass.

For a moment Fifi couldn't believe that she had heard him right, then she started to laugh hysterically. He stared at her over the rim of the glass.

"What's so damn funny?"

She managed to control herself a little.

"This weekend, your ex-mistress discovered she was pregnant by you and, as her husband is impotent, she can't pass it off as his."

Ian looked stunned. Then said "the stupid bitch! Hasn't she ever heard of the pill?"

Ignoring the interruption, Fifi continued.

"This same weekend I was given a telephone-book-length list of names of women you've gone to bed with during our marriage, and this weekend I have decided to ask for a divorce. And you say 'it went off very well'."

"Fifi," he groaned, "you don't really want a divorce. Alright, I admit to being a shit. But we've been happy for years. You don't want to throw all that away for one little misdemeanour."

"Not for one, no. I didn't, for one, if you can remember that far back. But when it gets into double figures, that's different."

He got up and walked over and sat on the arm of her chair. She felt the familiar warmth of his body, smelled the much-loved familiar smell that emanated from him, and felt her heart contract.

"None of them meant anything, darling." He put his arm round her shoulders.

"They do to me," she cried, and then shouted angrily at him. "Nobody ever meant anything to you, and I am not going to be insulted, humiliated, used and hurt by you ever again. I'll be better off alone." And, crying, she rushed from the room, and locked herself in Camilla's bedroom.

A few hours later, Ian came and tapped lightly on the door.

"Come downstairs and have some soup, you'll feel better then. We can watch a little TV. Then I'll have to start packing."

"I'll do it," she called out in a creaky voice.

She had always done his packing. Putting his shoes lovingly in initialled bags, padding the sleeves of his suit jackets so that they wouldn't be too creased, packing the business shirts separately from the leisure shirts, so that he knew exactly where to find everything. Everything Fifi had ever done for him she had done with loving care. He had been the one stable element in her life, and she had nothing with which to shore up this leaning tower. He had left his suitcase open on the bed ready for her. She packed automatically yet thinking, as she laid each item down, this is the last time, this is the last time, someone else will be doing it for him from now on. She had no doubt that Ian would find someone else to do everything for him.

They had the soup that he had heated, and a sandwich he had made with the rest of the roast beef, as they sat in front of the TV. It might have been any other Sunday night except for the fact that neither of them spoke. Fifi felt too empty to speak, and Ian was afraid he might say something that would break the apparent truce.

Going upstairs to bed, she turned and asked:

"What time shall I call you?"

"I have to leave by 7.30."

"6.15 then, is that all right?"

"Perfect."

Fifi opened the door to Camilla's room and he said, "Fifi, I really do love you. We'll have a long talk about it when I get back. I'll make it up to you. What we have is too precious to lose."

"We don't have anything," Fifi answered dully. "No loyalty, no trust, no honesty, no love, and, apparently, if your behaviour is anything to go by, no lust."

Then she closed the door firmly and locked it again.

At least she was talking to him, he thought. That must be a hopeful sign. No, all was not lost. When he was gone she would talk it over with the children. They wouldn't want the family broken up. It would work itself out. Satisfied, he lifted the suitcase off the bed, yawned, stretched and fell asleep.

6

First thing Monday morning there was little time to brood. Fifi woke to the sound of the alarm, feeling that she had not slept at all. Her pillow was wet with tears shed, she concluded, during a nightmare that had yet been an improvement on real life. Fearful that in her exhausted state she might drift back into sleep, she sprang from the bed so quickly that she developed hiccups as a result. Completely disorientated, she just brushed her hair and teeth, pulled on a dressing gown and stumbled downstairs to get Ian's tea.

Ian had slept well. He followed his usual pre-travel routine. Showered, shaved, dressed, checked that all his papers were in order. This meeting saw the culmination of all the company's ambitions. For a change, nothing had been leaked to the press, even though it was going to be the biggest trans-Atlantic amalgamation of the century. Ian felt like dancing round the bedroom. The big day had finally arrived and no slipups, and he, Ian Fraser Banners, was going to become the Managing Director of one of the largest companies in Europe.

It wasn't until he sat at the breakfast table and noticed that Fifi had not bothered to put on her 'morning' face, and was still in her dressing gown, that he remembered the crisis in his household. It slightly dampened his exuberance, but not entirely. Still, it did encourage him to share a little business information with her, something he had never been tempted to do before.

"If this meeting wasn't so terribly important to our company – and another which shall be nameless," he began, "I would have cancelled, so that we could get this personal problem sorted out. But we're signing an enormous deal, and so much depends on it. It'll alter my position substantially, and it'll make Geoffrey's life less fraught. The rat race is for younger men."

He paused to let that sink in, and to gauge her reaction at this choice bit of news, but there was none.

"It's still an absolute secret," he added urgently, "so you won't tell anyone else, will you?"

"I don't know anyone who would be interested," she answered dully.

As usual he left his typed itinerary on the kitchen pinboard, flight numbers and times, dates, hotel and telephone number. Ian made a move to kiss her as he left; unkempt as she appeared to be, he felt a surprising upsurge of tenderness towards her. He wanted to leave with her blessing as he had always done before, but she drew away from him.

"We'll keep this coming weekend just to ourselves. No visitors, no golf, just us. It will be like old times, and we'll thrash things out between us," was his parting shot.

Fifi closed the front door and went to the telephone, directed by some inner compulsion. Her movements were lethargic and she thought with panic, "I'm coming down with something. I mustn't let go now, though I feel so ill. I must get organised. Does one announce a forthcoming divorce like a wedding? Why haven't I paid attention to these things?"

Lifting the receiver she dialled the number of Percy's house at Eton, wondering if they would be at breakfast. They were, but Fifi told whoever answered that she had to speak to Percy on urgent family business.

Almost at once his housemaster took the phone.

"Good morning, Lady Florence. I don't wish to intrude in any way, but is the 'family business' something I should be acquainted with? Something that might cause Percy some grief, like a death?"

Fifi explained as best she could, adding, "I want to tell him myself. I was afraid he might see it in the papers and it would be a shock for him."

There was a hissing intake of breath.

"We do not allow those sort of papers here," came an offended, disapproving voice.

Equally offended, Fifi replied:

"Neither do I. I was not referring to the tabloids. I meant *The Times*."

"Ah, well, I see. They've finally managed to locate your son now. Here he is. Please don't keep him too long."

Percy's surprisingly adult voice said, "Hello, Mummy. Am I being expelled?"

"What for?"

"Ah, well, if you don't know, then it must be all right."

"I hope so. I don't think I could stand anything extra today."

"It's nice to hear from you anyway."

"You probably won't think so. I telephoned to tell you that Daddy and I are getting a divorce."

After only a second's silence, he said, "But I can still live with you, can't I?"

"Of course you can, and will, darling. I wouldn't have it any other way. But Im afraid it will have to be a flat in town."

"Smashing. Where?"

"I don't know yet."

"Can I have a bed that folds into the wall, like Garner's? He never has to make it. It smells like a hamster's cage."

"Is that good?" Fifi actually laughed. "Yes, you can have one if I can find one."

Percy was delighted. His friends had always told him divorce was a good thing, and Fifi sounded in the right mood for a touch.

"By the way, Mummy, I'm a little short this week. Bad management I'm afraid. Could you surreptitiously slip a fiver or, better still, a tenner, into my letter this week? I'd be ever so grateful."

Fifi was grateful too, for the fact that he could make her smile under these circumstances, that he was so normal, and obvious. Perhaps a tenner would put right whatever it was he thought he might be expelled for.

"Alright, a tenner," Fifi agreed, "But this once only. So don't push your luck in the future."

"Smashing!" exclaimed Percy again enthusiastically. "Thanks. I'll see you at the next exeat, won't I?"

"Yes, at Granny's, which is where you can reach me if you need me."

Fifi sat for a moment contemplating the telephone. She had been surprised that Percy had sounded so normal when, for her, everything was changed.

She dialled William's digs in Exeter. A sleepy male voice answered.

"May I speak to William Bannerss, please," she asked politely.

"Eh? What time is it?"

Fifi glanced at the grandfather clock. It was 8.15. Too late now to telephone Camilla in London, she would have left for work. She was always the first one there, determined to make herself indispensable. So strange for a twenty year-old.

"It's 8.15," Fifi informed the voice.

"Oh, Christ. I've got a tutorial at 8.30."

The phone bumped and banged against the wall at William's end where it had been dropped and left to dangle. Fifi was trying to decide what to do, whether to hang up and try again, or hang on. Before she had decided, William's voice floated up to her.

"William," Fifi cried with relief, "I wasn't sure if your friend had called you."

"He's not my friend any more. I was in bed with a lovely popsy."

"William! this is your mother," protested Fifi.

"Only joking, Ma. What's the problem?"

"What newspaper do you read?"

"Are you conducting a survey, or has Dad been caught with his hand in the till?'

"No, but he has been found in a few extra-marital beds. I'm divorcing him."

"Good for you. Are you all right?"

"Yes, dear. I think so," but his ready sympathy already brought the prickle of tears to her eyes, and a thickening in her throat.

31

"Will you be OK financially?"

"Oh, yes."

"Will I?" William was very aware of his dependency on Ian for financial help.

"Oh, William, of course you will. This won't change how your father feels about you."

"That's not very encouraging. I don't think he feels any more for us than any of his other possessions. All replaceable."

Years of keeping a united front, of remembering "not in front of the children, or the servants", if one had any, brought the response. "You mustn't think things like that," she said, still loyal to her principles. "You will be absolutely safe financially, I'll guarantee that."

"I accept that. Is the summer holiday still on?"

Fifi and Ian had always taken a villa with a swimming pool for the summer holidays, and each member of the family could bring a friend to stay. They had talked of Tuscany this year, but Fifi had wanted to go back to the Algarve.

"Yes, of course it is. You're all welcome to stay with me, as usual. I thought the Algarve this year. The weather is always beautiful."

"Right. I'll line someone up."

"I'm thinking of inviting Granny too. She has friends at Vale de Lobo."

After a moment's hesitation, William asked nervously.

"She won't be bringing someone my age, will she?"

Fifi stifled a laugh. The children's responses to her mother's toyboys were cold.

"No. I expect if she wants someone your age she'll make do with your friend."

"Wrong sex. Tough luck. Bye," and William quickly hung up. Suddenly, for no apparent reason, Fifi began to cry. She put her head down on the telephone and sobbed aloud.

That was how Gladys found her when she came in at nine o'clock. Cradling Fifi against her bony bosom, she urged her back upstairs, only to be met with a blank refusal when it came to entering her own room. Fifi knew it would still smell of Ian, his aftershave in the bathroom, his hair on the pillow, his much-loved body on the sheets. It was as if he had died and she both wanted to be with him, and yet could not bear any reminders.

Gladys covered her up in Camilla's room, noting the already-slept-in bed, and got the whole story out of her.

"Not Mrs Martin too? Oh, what a wicked woman!" gasped Gladys.

"I don't suppose she was any worse than Mrs Hatton."

"Yes, but they're London people. They don't know any better. I think I should get her ladyship to come down and fetch you back."

"No. No," protested Fifi, "I couldn't face her."

"Rubbish. That's what mothers are for, or – " Gladys stopped, suddenly struck with one of her brilliant ideas. "What about Mrs Francis? I'm sure she would never have had any nonsense with him, and she's been a friend of yours for years, and divorced three times, so she'll know just what to do."

"That's it, Gladys. You're brilliant. I'll phone Carol. She'll be able to help me." Fifi threw back the duvet and ran into her bedroom.

Ignoring Ian's invisible presence, she went to the telephone. As soon as she heard Carol's happy voice, "Fifi, how lovely! Where are you? In town?" her resolve deserted her. In a quavering voice she just managed to say, "Oh. Carol, it's the end of the world," before bursting into tears again.

Gladys snatched the phone and explained, ending with, "And she's been so brave, coping with it all over the weekend, never letting on, but now it's really hit her hard."

"She's going to have to cope a little longer," Carol said firmly. "Get her a pencil and paper, she has a lot to do. I shall be down as soon as I can after lunch. Put her back on the line."

"Now," Carol ordered, "pull yourself together, Madam. I shall be down to fetch you at about 3.00. In the meantime, you are to have a shower and get dressed in something comfortable. Then pack two suitcases with clothes for the moment, plus any trinkets, jewellery and little homely things like the children's pictures. Collect any important papers, your passport, birth certificates, etc., bank book – Do you have a joint account?"

"We each have our own personal accounts, and a joint one."

"Right. When you've finished packing go to the bank and clean out the joint account. It will give you a float. Have you any evidence?"

"Evidence?"

"Letters, bills, receipts from hotels, cheque stubs, photos of Ian with any of the women?"

"No evidence like that. Ian would never have incriminated himself and, if he had, he wouldn't have kept anything like that here."

"Don't you believe it," said Carol. "Cowboys put notches on their guns, pygmies wear shrunken heads, Indians have scalps on their belts, and the average man keeps a record of his success with women, to gloat over in the impotent years, or for a nostalgic quick look back when his ego needs boosting. Ian must have a private drawer that he keeps locked."

"Yes, he has. But I'm sure it's full of business papers."

"Yes, dirty business. Real business is kept at the office. Get it open and go through it with a fine-tooth comb. If you can't find anything, I'll go through it when I arrive."

"I can't go through his things, Carol. I shall feel such a sneak."

"Does he? School days are over, Fifi, face life. Now off you go. Put crushed ice on your eyelids, or cucumber, while Gladys goes up to the attic for your cases."

"It's all right. There are two cases in the hall cupboard."

"You'll need more than two. During the week, Gladys is going to have to pack all your personal things and have them sent up before Ian gets back. I'll explain it all to you when I get there. Gird your loins now, and get started. Eyes first, money next, then packing."

With the decisions being made for her Fifi found the strength to do as she had been ordered. Gladys made her stop for lunch, which she ate like an obedient child, and then turned her attention to Ian's long desk drawer. It was locked tight, but she had seen him close and lock it many times. Standing in the middle of the room she tried to visualise him putting the big bunch of keys away. He had never tried to do it secretly. He had trusted her completely, as well he might. Visualising him was a painful process. He sprang to life in her mind, his pristine shirt, his taut buttocks neatly encased in well-tailored trousers – she had always loved the way his strong calves pushed at the legs of his trousers. In her mind he turned and smiled at her as he had done so often in the bedroom, and she had melted before he even touched her. That wonderful smile that lit up his grey eyes and crinkled his tanned face. Her resolution crumbled, her lips trembled.

"I can't do it," she mumbled, "I can't."

Gladys didn't realise Fifi meant that she couldn't leave him. She thought Fifi was too honest to look in his drawer.

"Well, don't you fret, love," she said. "We can always get young Susie's father to give evidence. He'd be glad of the chance."

"Young Susie?"

"You mean you didn't know? Oh dear, what have I gone and said?"

"You'd better finish now, Gladys."

"It was Susie Robinson, the young barmaid at The Bull. Mr Bannerss got her in the family way. Mr Robinson demanded money for her. Mr Bannerss didn't want to pay, he said it could have been anybody's. Out of respect for you Mr Robinson didn't come up here, but he went to Mr Martin, knowing he was Mr Banners's solicitor, and Mr Martin arranged for her to have a thousand pounds. She went away and had the kid, and had it adopted. She's back now, but everyone round here knows she's damaged goods."

Fifi was appalled. She remembered the girl, though not by name. She had looked about the same age as Camilla. The shock of this disclosure gave her the impetus necessary to try once more to locate the keys. She closed her eyes again and immediately remembered which drawer they were in.

As Carol had speculated, the drawer was full of "dirty business". Hotel receipts for Mr and Mrs Bannersss, always at the Grand Hotel, either in Eastbourne, or Brighton or Bognor, no hole-in-the-wall one-night stands for him. The cheque stubs revealed how generous he had been over the years during an affair, and he had not stinted on holidays for them either. The hardest things to bear were the pictures. They were all similar. Ian sitting naked on a dressing table stool in front of a mirror with a naked woman on his lap. He had obviously taken the snaps himself, one hand between the woman's thighs as he and she said "sex" to the lens. There was Janice, Mandy, "Mandy Welch!" thought Fifi in surprise. He had always said she was deformed, but she didn't look deformed in the picture, and there was nothing hidden. Joan King, that nice secretary Ian had had for two years, and others she didn't know. So many women, some looking coy, some lewd, and some embarrassed. There were pictures of Ian at the Lido in Paris, the Stork Club in New York, at the Beach Club in Bermuda, at the Casino in Monte Carlo, all with different women. Fifi put them all into her suitcase with the cheque stubs and receipts. She was numb. Had she ever known him? Ian had been her husband for twenty-three years, so who was this stranger?

Carol arrived, brisk, with a no-nonsense manner. She conferred with Gladys, applauded Fifi's finds, went through all Ian's suit pockets, dressing gowns, towelling robes, jackets, then said jauntily, "Let's have a quick cup of tea and be off. You have a solicitor's appointment tomorrow morning at 10.30 while it's still fresh in your mind."

"I can't talk to a stranger about something so personal," wailed Fifi.

"Ron Matthews isn't a stranger, Fifi. He's a divorce lawyer, and your best friend. He understands everything. You won't have to volunteer anything. He'll ask questions, and you just answer. He's so kind. I know how you feel. I'm the wounded veteran of three wars myself."

36

Fifi left some money with Gladys for small local bills, to send on her luggage, and in case Ian forgot to pay her for the week. He had never previously had to concern himself with the mundane matters of the household.

As they drove off, Carol asked, "Do the children know?"

"William and Percy do. Camilla leaves for work too early for me to have contacted her this morning. It isn't the sort of thing I'd like to tell her on the office phone."

"No," agreed Carol. "Never mind, you can phone her from the flat and let her know where you are."

Wrapped in misery, Fifi started what was to be the long journey back to self-respect.

7

Fifi signed the heart-stopping cheque, 'Florence Irene Bannerss', with a flourish. It seemed to her that the entire travel agency was holding its breath as she did so. It was the first time in twenty-three years that she had booked a holiday without first consulting Ian – about the place, the cost, the accommodation – not that he had ever evinced any real interest, but he would have been furious if he had felt that he didn't have the right to veto everything. He was, as he often boasted, the "head" of the house. Fifi had never considered the fact that as she did all the booking, packing and arranging, she was really entitled to the final say. From now on things were going to be different.

She stood up, a lean, fragile-looking figure, with a mop of brown wavy hair hanging loosely to her shoulders. She felt empty, light-headed. It was a strange feeling, younger, as if her clothes fitted better. She smiled at the young counter clerk.

"Is that everything now?"

The girl smiled back.

"Yes, Lady Florence. I'll telephone you when the tickets and papers are ready."

Fifi went out onto the street and hailed a passing taxi. She gave her parents' address in the Boltons.

When the cab stopped she felt her heart sink. Still, it had to be faced. They probably already knew. She couldn't imagine Ian not phoning them to complain as soon as he found out she was not there to serve his dinner, press his city suit, and get his breakfast.

In half of this she was proved right. Her father was in his morning room. As soon as Martin, the butler, showed her in he shouted at her in an aggrieved voice.

"Where have you been? That husband of yours has been

telephoning constantly for you. Why he thought you were here I cannot imagine. A wife should be where her husband can reach her."

"Why?" asked Fifi, to infuriate her father. He spluttered and coughed. His face almost purple. His foot was raised on a small stool and he looked every minute of his eighty-one years. Her mind registered that he had gout again as he shouted:

"Because that's what wives are supposed to do!"

"Not any more," Fifi told him calmly. "Ian and I are getting a divorce. At least, I am."

For a moment the Earl of Cheswick was speechless, a very rare occurrence during his waking hours, but these too were getting fewer since gout, impotence and ill-temper had caught up with him. When he finally opened his mouth he said exactly what Fifi had expected.

"I suppose your mother put you up to this."

Fifi shook her head.

"Thea doesn't know yet."

This gave him another reason to start a tirade.

"Do not refer to your mother by her Christian name. I won't have any of those new-fangled, disrespectful ideas in my house."

"Father," said Fifi with a deep sigh, "I am forty-three years old. I have grown-up children of my own, and no longer expect to be told how to behave by you."

This statement, instead of quieting him, only gave him a new angle to argue.

"I'm glad you've remembered your children. What will the boys think? They're at an impressionable age – it will be terribly upsetting for them."

"It won't make any difference to them at all. I've spoken to William at Exeter."

"I can imagine how shocked he was. Have you taken leave of your senses?"

"No, I've just come to them. And he wasn't shocked. I asked him what newspaper he took and he asked, 'Why, has the old man been caught with his fingers in the till?' When I explained, he just said, 'Oh, right! Will it affect my allowance?' I said no, and he said, 'good-o' and rang off."

"Well, it's all right for him. I mean Exeter, that's hardly the sort of place where they do things properly. My thoughts go out to young Percy. Divorce is hardly the 'done' thing at Eton."

Fifi couldn't fight the urge to laugh.

"Father, the world has changed since you were a boy. I've spoken to Percy also. He was delighted. Apparently he is the only boy in his class who's had the same two parents all his life. I rang off whilst he was urging me to marry someone famous as soon as I could. In any case, I wasn't worried about him. Anyone who can survive school with a name like Percy can survive anything. It's Camilla I have been worrying about. She used to adore Ian and I'm so afraid he'll play on her sympathy and drag her down to look after him until the house is sold."

"He can't sell the house. Where will he live? A chap can hardly live at his club, people would talk."

"Frankly I don't care where he lives. My solicitor says I am entitled to half the value of the house, at least, and I want it."

"I can see that Ian has dragged you down into the commercial world he inhabits. When you lived at home you would never have been so vulgar."

"Vulgar? What have I said that is vulgar?"

"You're talking about money. Decent people don't talk about money. Ring the bell. I want a drink."

"So do I," agreed Fifi, and she pressed the button by the fireplace.

Martin appeared immediately, proving that he still listened outside the doors, so that nothing took place in the house without him knowing of it.

"I want a whisky and soda," announced the Earl petulantly.

"And so do I," Fifi added.

"Wouldn't you prefer a sherry?" enquired the Earl, clinging to a last forlorn hope that Fifi might become once more the amenable, apologetic girl who had left this house on her wedding day.

She shook her head.

"Make mine a double, Martin," she ordered, "with ice. I've earned it."

"Putting ice in whisky is . . . is . . ." her father searched for a suitably censorious word.

"So vulgar?" suggested Fifi.

She snatched the glass from the tray Martin proffered and waltzed over to the door.

"I'll take it up and drink it with Thea, in case her reaction is the same as yours," and she kicked off her shoes in the hall and skipped up the marble stairs.

8

Thea was sitting at her satin skirted dressing table in a beige satin slip, contemplating ten different pairs of earrings. She looked young for her sixty-two years. Her short hair was that indeterminate blonde so popular with hairdressers when faced with a client with white hair who refuses to have it blue. Thea had been able to give her hairdresser a good reason for her reluctance. During their childhood her only brother, Adrian, had been given a grey pony with a white mane and tail, and, whilst he had been dressing up for events, Thea had been commandeered into making a solution with a Rickets Blue Bag and water, and combed it carefully through the pony's mane and tail until the right silvery colour had resulted. The only thanks she had ever received was a truculent "not bad" from Adrian as he had ridden off to some gymkhana or other. So, whenever Thea saw blue hair, her mind automatically registered "horse", and she was determined not to end up looking like a horse; not that that would have been very possible since her teeth were inclined to slope inwards and not outwards, as befits a horse, and her face was round and soft, with round, startled blue eyes; more kittenish than horsey.

Without looking up she said, "Welcome, darling. What a lovely surprise," as Fifi came in.

"How did you know it was me?" Fifi exclaimed, adding as she stuck out her stockinged foot, "I didn't make a sound."

"Your perfume preceded you."

"Yes. Oh, damn it. I've been using the same one for years and now, suddenly, it reacts differently on my skin. It gets stronger and stronger."

"It's your hormones. As we get older we need lighter perfumes."

"Back to youth and lavender water, I suppose," sighed Fifi.

"More likely, on to the change and HRT," said Thea.

"Thanks a lot." Fifi put her drink down on the dressing table and sank into the blue satin chair beside it. Thea sniffed her glass.

"Whisky? You must be feeling exhausted."

Fifi nodded.

"I am and of course Pa hasn't improved matters. I came to tell you both that I've left Ian. I'm divorcing him."

"Darling! How absolutely wonderful. I've always wondered how you could stand seeing him at breakfast every morning. He is the most boring man I've ever met, and I have met quite a few."

Then she stretched out her hand and put it comfortingly over Fifi's.

"Are you alright, Fifi? You know you can count on me for anything."

When Fifi had been small Thea had been an affectionate, demonstrative mother, full of hugs and kisses, but she had been shamed out of it by her mother-in-law's shocked disgust, Nanny's frowns and her husband's disapproval. Now she found it difficult to show her love for Fifi in any physical way. She felt too self-conscious. Fifi understood.

"Yes, I do know," she replied putting her free hand over her mother's, "and I'm fine. I feel enormously relieved. I feel liberated. A little frightened, as though I'm holding my breath. It's hard to explain."

"You don't need to explain," Thea practically snapped. "You're well rid of him."

Fifi was surprised at the vehemence in Thea's voice.

"Did you know he was unfaithful?"

"Given half a chance," Thea replied with a sigh, "all men are unfaithful."

"Oh, no. Surely not all of them," protested Fifi.

"Well, I suppose some drink instead."

Fifi laughed.

"Into which one of these categories does Pa fit?"

"As if you didn't know."

"So why didn't you divorce him?"

Having finally decided on the tiger's head earrings with the emerald eyes, Thea put them on, then wandered over to the bed and picked up her skirt.

"Things were different when I was younger. I was eighteen when I married Guy. He was a widower and I thought he needed comforting, and companionship. He had a title, money and was near to forty. Granny thought he was a catch, that he would be grateful for my youth and look after me. Ha! He was unfaithful on our honeymoon, and never looked back. I asked for a divorce after you were born. He said I could go but that if I did, I should never see you again, and I believed that he had that much power. He said a judge would laugh his little infidelities out of court, everyone knew that men were different. Of course, I had no criteria to go by. My father had died when I was eight, so I accepted his word, but I never let him in my bed again. Do you know that the night you were being born, he spent with another woman and then, instead of visiting me in the hospital, he took her to the races. When he finally deigned to see me he was hurt that I should take him to task for it. He said I should be grateful for the rest, and that he had put the birth announcement in the *Times* for me. I argued that it would have been better to wait until we'd decided on a name, and he said he already had. He had named you after his mother, Florence Irene, as if I had no rights at all."

"Is that why I've always been called Fifi?"

Thea nodded.

"I didn't mind the Irene, Irene was the Greek Goddess of Peace, but Florence! The old cat came to see me and tell me to stop 'carrying on like a downstairs servant'. She said Guy would be much more attentive next time, when I had a boy. I was so cross I told her that Guy wasn't going to use me as a baby machine whilst he entertained any tart he fancied."

Thea laughed at the memory.

"She swept out, but Guy and I have lived separate lives ever since. He wouldn't consider a divorce – such a scandal, my dear, and once or twice he offered me bribes to give him an heir, and then threats, but neither worked. I'd enlisted Granny's aid by then and knew where I stood. Will you be all right financially?"

"I've seen a solicitor who says I will. I'm entitled to half of everything. And I have some shares and money put by. I suppose I shall get used to managing alone."

"You'll love it. Such freedom. Of course it's different for me. I feel I am living in a first class hotel. I don't have to organise anything except the occasional dinner party or hunt weekend, and my allowance is paid into my account with embarrassing regularity considering I don't do anything for it. I don't even know if Guy has the money to do it. I shall probably be asked to pay it all back when he dies."

Fifi looked shocked.

"Don't you know what arrangements he's made? Suppose a third cousin twice removed turns up and claims the house and title?"

"Don't be silly," laughed Thea, "Your William will inherit. He'll have the title, and Cheswick Manor – to which he is welcome – but this house is mine. Granny insisted on that when we married. She said a gentleman always gave his wife a house; her husband had only been a baronet but he had seen to it that she had a house, and the wherewithal to maintain it. Guy was always so anxious to prove to her what a gentleman he was, so I have the house."

A discreet tap on the door deferred further conversation and a sleek blond head sporting a long pageboy bob peered round.

"Are you decent? Can I come in? I'm in," and a tall, tanned young man in his late twenties, wearing a pale beige suit with a black shirt, and a beige tie with blue gentians on it, appeared.

"Darling!" he exclaimed as Thea did up her black blouse. "We're twins."

He went and stood beside her, tweaking first her blouse and then his own shirt. "What do you think?" he asked Fifi.

"But not Siamese twins," trilled Thea. "Mark, this is my daughter, Fifi."

"Yes, I can see where you get your looks from, Thea," Mark said, smiling. "Hi, Fifi."

"Fifi, this is Mark. He's taking me out tonight, somewhere very expensive."

"Oh, God forbid. I hope not," protested Mark. "I thought I was your toyboy. Toyboys get taken."

"To bed, not to eat," teased Thea, and then hurriedly apologised to Fifi. "So sorry, darling, that's not mother talk, is it? Are you shocked?"

Fifi laughed.

"I'll try not to be."

"I see it all now. I am covered with shame and contrition," said Mark. "Fifi is a refugee from a convent. I promise that henceforth no lewd remarks will pass my lips."

With a final look in the long mirror, Thea put her arm round Fifi's shoulders.

"You see why I can't resist him. He makes me laugh. Let's go downstairs and have a drink with grumpy Guy before we go out. Then he can't say other wives entertain their husbands more than I do."

Fifi let them walk ahead of her down the stairs, as she was afraid of slipping in her stockinged feet. When they reached the bottom and turned back to look at her, she couldn't help laughing as they stood side by side in their identical outfits.

"Are you sure you didn't plan these outfits?" she asked.

"I never plan anything," said Mark.

"Two minds with but a single thought," insisted Thea.

Guy greeted Mark with, "You ought to get a haircut."

Mark was not offended. He pulled his hair into a ponytail at the back and answered,

"It's Mozart year, and I have been wearing it tied back with a black bow. Out of deference to you, Sir, I decided not to wear it. Mozart being German and all that."

There was no particular reason why something German

should have upset Guy, but hearing the word deference put him in a good mood and they had more than one drink before exiting.

They shared a taxi, and Mark and Thea dropped Fifi at the corner of New Cavendish Street and Marylebone High Street, which was only a couple of steps away from the entrance to Carol's flat.

9

Feeling almost happy, and definitely slightly tipsy, Fifi walked up New Cavendish Street. Arriving outside the block of flats, she was surprised to find the large front doors closed. Then she remembered that Carol had warned her that the porter closed the door when he went off duty at 6 p.m., leaving the residents to let themselves in with their own keys.

Fumbling in her bag she discovered the key and slipped the bag firmly back under her arm, but, as she turned the key in the lock, an arm came over her shoulder and pushed the door open for her. She turned, startled, and saw a well-dressed, clean-shaven man standing there. Thinking he must be one of the other residents, she thanked him politely. He muttered, "You're welcome," as he waited for her to enter ahead of him, then he followed her to the lift.

"Which floor is yours?" she asked.

She turned towards him as she spoke, thus escaping the full force of the blow he aimed at her with something small, round, and in a sock. It caught her on the cheek instead of the back of the head, but the force of it sent her reeling backwards, hitting her head against the lift wall, at the same time as he tried to wrench her handbag from her grasp. She had the strap over her shoulder and automatically clung to it. Furiously, he struck out and hit her on the shoulder and again on the face. Terrified, not able to think what to do to evade the blows, Fifi kicked out with her stiletto-heeled shoes. She heard the hard impact as the heel met his shin bone. He yelped and stepped backwards. With all her force she pushed him from the lift, hoping to close the metal door quickly and escape, but the strap of her handbag broke, and it fell, spilling the contents onto the floor. Lipstick, pen, compact, glasses case, cheque book, comb, Kleenex and aspirin dispersed noisily on to the tiles. Her assailant hesitated, looked down to see if there was anything worth grabbing, saw no wallet or purse – Fifi always kept those in the zipped pocket of her bags – and turned and fled, leaving the front door open behind him.

Dazed, Fifi stared after him. Her mind instructed her to close the front door, but she couldn't bring herself to cross the wide, empty expanse of the hall, supposing that he might be waiting outside the door ready to pounce on her again. She sank to her knees, hardly conscious of what she was doing, and began to collect the scattered contents of her handbag. After feeling blindly about her to be sure she had missed nothing, she staggered back into the lift and pressed the third-floor button.

Leaning against the wall for support, she made her way along the long corridor to Carol's flat. She just stood there with her finger on the bell.

Carol was shouting, "I'm coming! Stop that bloody racket!" as she came to open the door. She took one surprised look, gasped, "What on earth has happened to you?" and dragged Fifi inside.

Once Carol had the story, she telephoned the police, and her doctor. Carol was informed that the emergency doctor would come as soon as he could. So they sat and waited, and waited. A quiet, gentle Indian doctor arrived eventually. He pronounced that there were no broken bones. He advised ice packs quickly to treat the facial bruises, and aspirin to soothe the pain of the others. Fifi shivered and sobbed as he talked.

"Let's get her to bed," the doctor suggested. "She is in shock. Have you blankets and hot water bottles? And a drink, not alcohol, a hot drink, preferably tea."

Once Fifi was wrapped up and recumbent, the doctor picked up his bag.

"I'll leave you a sedative for her tonight, you won't want to go out and get a prescription filled and leave her alone in this state. Some women have less resistance to distress than others."

"Fifi is average, I think, but she's already had one bad shock this week," Carol replied, and then explained.

To her surprise the doctor immediately put his bag down again and went in and sat on Fifi's bed. She was lying, white and dishevelled, hugging the hot water bottle with one arm and holding the ice pack to her cheek with the other.

"It is a common phenomenon that people who are going through one emotional crisis attract other crises," the doctor began. "They become more accident prone, more liable to suffer other traumas, even cancers. It is as if the first injury has set up a chain reaction. To overcome this you must divest yourself of all worldly adornments. Take them off now and put them under your pillow. Earrings, watch, bracelets, necklets, even your wedding ring."

Mesmerised, Fifi did as he told her.

"Now you must put your self in a state of suspended animation. Blank out all your thoughts. Then meditate, let your mind take you where it will. Dream, let yourself go free."

Carol stared at him in amazement. She was used to the five minute appointments schedule at the surgery, the "rush in, rush out, have a pill" treatment. As far as she knew, Dr Singh was not even a member of the group practice, and yet he was taking all this time with Fifi, and it was helping. Fifi was listening to him with fascination, her pain and misery momentarily forgotten.

"I can't," she protested, "my mind is in such a muddle, I can't even think straight."

"That is what I meant. When the mind has lost its path you are endangered. You must catch hold of it, nurse it, steer it back to stillness. Try this. Close your eyes, transport yourself to a lovely beach beside a sunlit sea. Listen to the lapping of the ripples on the shore, watch the sea birds, see the breeze moving the fronds of the palm trees. Lie in the sun you have created, rest, recuperate, sleep, sleep, sleep."

Fifi never moved as the doctor got up quietly.

"Don't forget more ice packs," he said to Carol as he left the bedroom.

Carol followed him, saying accusingly. "I was almost asleep, are you a hypnotist?"

"Must everything have a name? Nameless diseases need nameless cures. If you need me again, the surgery has my number. Keep her quiet and warm, and remind her from time to time that there are other worlds, less turbulent worlds. People tied up to this world miss the chance to find their own world."

Carol didn't have much time for the mysticism of the East, but, against her will, she was impressed by Doctor Singh. When she let him out she found two plain clothes policemen waiting at the door. They recognised Doctor Singh immediately.

"What's the damage?" one of them asked him brusquely.

"Intensive bruising and shock. She is calm now, but don't stay too long."

With great self-control they omitted to remark that they had no time to waste either.

Fifi tried to concentrate on their questions, but all she wanted to do was sleep, which they wouldn't allow.

They asked the colour of her attacker, and what he was wearing. Then they told her that there was a mugging every three minutes in London, motivated as much by hate and spite, as by poverty and necessity. They told her how lucky she had been not having sustained serious injury, or lost a lot of money. They said also that they would try and apprehend her assailant, but didn't hold out much hope.

When they left, Fifi's lovely image of a deserted, sun-drenched beach had completely evaporated.

10

Later, Fifi sat with a packet of frozen peas pressed to her purple cheek, balefully eyeing Carol from out of her slightly swollen eye. Carol started to laugh.

"Forgive me, Fifi. I am sorry. I know it isn't funny, but you do look funny," she spluttered. "You have to admit that when you do fall apart, you certainly do it wholeheartedly."

Fifi who felt quite hysterical, began to laugh also, but stopped as suddenly as she had started.

"Oh, ouch! That hurts!" she exclaimed, "and it's not me that's fallen apart, it's my life. It isn't worth living any more. My husband never gave a damn about me, and now total strangers are seeking me out in the street to batter. It isn't fair! There aren't any nice people left."

"There's me," Carol corrected her indignantly.

"Granted, there's you, but I would still like to go away somewhere, and live on another planet."

The telephone rang and Carol left the room to answer it. She spoke only briefly and then returned.

"I think going to another planet is a very good idea. Failing a planet a country retreat would do. That was a friend of mine on the phone, she works for a gossip columnist. They've just had the word on the grapevine – which means a paid informer at some police station – that Lady Florence Bannerss, staying at this address, fought off a mugger this evening. She said all the dirty dailies will be round here in the morning. So we'd better be somewhere else."

"Oh, God! That's all I need on top of everything else. A scandal! Pa will never speak to me again. I can't bear it."

But Carol was no longer listening. She was back at the telephone with her telephone book on her lap.

52

Left alone, Fifi sank back on the pillows and dozed off. Carol, dressed in a track suit, woke her.

"Rise and shine, Fifi. I've packed a few things for you, but you'll have to pack your face yourself. We're off to a health farm."

"Now? In the middle of the night?"

"It's no longer the middle of the night. It's dawn. We have to hurry before the press arrive and smell dirt. They will, you know, because you're here without Ian, and not at the Boltons with your ever-loving parents."

The explanation was wasted on Fifi, whose muddled head was sinking back onto the pillow. She mumbled, "No one would let us in at this hour. Besides, you have to reserve at those places, they're like hotels."

"Quite true. But I happen to have already stayed at a couple of them, and know someone. It always pays to know someone. I tried to get us into Ragdale Hall, because it's a long way from here, and they have a flotation tank, which is something I've never tried, but their first vacancy was next Monday. Come on, Fifi!" She pulled back the covers. "Get up – NOW. I've booked us into Champneys, at Tring. They have a stress counsellor, which you may need. You'll probably end up having to pay for me too because it's madly expensive, and my new bank manager is not as friendly as the last."

"I would pay anything for you, Carol." Fifi crawled painfully out of bed. "You're the best friend anyone could ever have. You've saved my sanity, and my life, and I don't deserve you."

"Rubbish! You'd do the same for me. In fact you have. We'll contact William and Camilla as soon as we get there, and your parents, so that the newspaper reports won't panic them, and they'll be able to reassure Percy when he sees it and telephones for news."

"I've been told they don't allow those sort of newspapers at Eton."

Carol laughed.

"I expect they do, and use them for loo paper."

In spite of the fact that it was only just daybreak, Champneys welcomed them. The night staff, who were still on duty, apologised for not being able to offer them separate rooms at such short notice.

The twin-bedded room reserved for them was big enough, the bathroom elegant. Unfortunately the mini-bar only contained mineral water, but there was a small electric kettle for hot drinks.

"Of what?" Fifi whispered as the attendant left their luggage. There were no sachets or tea bags visible. Carol put her fingers to her lips mysteriously, then opened her suitcase. A jar of instant coffee appeared, then sachets for hot chocolate, tea bags, and half bottles of whisky and gin. These Carol quickly put into a drawer and covered with sweat shirts.

"These are prohibited, usually," she explained. Fifi found a note on the dressing table confirming appointments for both of them with the doctor that morning. No treatments were allowed before that, not even a facial, the note said.

"I shall never want a facial again," groaned Fifi, her cheek a sore, swollen bruise in spite of the ice packs. "When I see the doctor, what shall I tell him?"

"Or her. There are women doctors, you know. Tell the truth. Say you've just been mugged, that you're getting a divorce, and you wish you were dead. Oh, my goodness!" she exclaimed laughing. "They'll probably think Ian's beaten you up."

"All the way from Bermuda?" asked Fifi as she collapsed onto the bed, and was asleep before Carol could even cover her up.

Fifi soon found out that the best thing about a health farm was the atmosphere of being completely removed from reality. Every minute of the day was filled with some personal attention or service. Fifi had never been so indulged and spoilt. She had saunas and body massages – her face was too tender to touch. She swam twice a day. She also had long talks with the stress counsellor, who advised her to look closely at her own reactions, to try and discover what had hurt her most about Ian's behaviour.

"I don't have to look, I know," Fifi insisted. "It was the sense of betrayal."

"His betrayal, or the woman's?"

"His, of course. I trusted him. I didn't mind being alone. I knew his work involved travelling, and that he loved it. I didn't mind being alone whilst he was alone – but not alone, whilst he was with someone else. With friends of mine." At this point Fifi always began to shake, to have to fight back the tears. "Brazenly, publicly, with friends of mine, and he never tried to hide it, except from me."

When asked if she had thrown things, screamed and shouted, she was shocked.

"I've never made a scene in my life," she replied. "I just walked out."

"Then you must still have a lot of unresolved anger building up inside you," suggested the counsellor.

"No, I feel calmer now than I've ever felt. It's just that I cry a lot." She looked shamefaced. "For no reason at all, I suddenly burst into tears. It's very embarrassing."

Fifi was given a book on meditation, but couldn't sit still long enough to read it. She could not concentrate on anything. She and Carol went for long walks together. They sat joking in the sauna together, always the same joke. Fifi, who had lost a lot of weight without trying, would say:

"I didn't know I had this much sweat in me."

To which Carol would reply, "Wait till you get the bill."

"It doesn't matter," Fifi said comfortingly, "The float can handle it."

The float was the money she had taken from the joint account. It pleased her to think that Ian was having to pay for Carol as well. She knew he didn't like Carol and it served him right.

Carol kept in touch with Thea, charting Fifi's progress. It would have been possible to return to the flat after the first week since interest in Fifi had died down almost immediately, but her mood swings were still so unpredictable that Thea encouraged Carol to keep her there longer.

The second week of their stay, Fifi showed a marked improvement, making plans for Percy's coming weekend at home, and discussing possibilities for her own future. Wrapped in a fluffy bathrobe, she discussed the openings that might be available with one of the resident physiotherapists. They were not encouraging.

"You won't get a job on National Health because they've really cut back so fiercely. You might get something at a private clinic, or a gym, but the hours at a gym are very long. There's work to be had at sports clubs," she was told.

"Would I need a refresher course?"

"I should jolly well think so after twenty years! There are so many new treatments available now. I'll make some enquiries for you if you like."

Carol was not enthusiastic for Fifi to even think of career decisions, or courses, until later.

"Don't try to run before you can walk, Fifi," she advised. "It's not over yet. You'll find you're up one day and down the next. Have your summer holiday, and then start to make plans. You'll be over the worst by September."

Fifi was beginning to feel ready for anything, but knew that Carol had had more experience than she had and that, at this moment, she was living in an unreal atmosphere.

They decided to travel back to London via Eton and pick Percy up for his exeat. He was surprised that Fifi had come herself.

"You might have phoned and said you were coming," he said accusingly. "All my friends wanted to hear the lurid details from your own lips. You don't look very beaten up to me."

Fifi, who had spent hours weeping at a desk as she tried to compose a cheerful weekly letter to him, something that would not upset him, was indignant.

"I wrote to you and explained what happened, and bruises don't last forever, thank goodness."

"I suppose not. Was he a skinhead? I shall be asked when I get back."

"No, he wasn't."

"I'd like to have my head shaved this summer. Smythson had his done and was sent home until it grew back again, but they can hardly say much in the hols. By the way, Dad sent me £50 for this exeat. He says I'm to take you out somewhere."

"That will be nice," Fifi replied without thinking. "Where shall we go?"

"Oh, Mumsy. Have you no couth? You are divorcing the man. The correct thing to say is, 'I don't want his money, you can keep it'."

Fifi exchanged smiles with Carol.

"Not a hope, young man. In fact we'll stop at the first McDonald's we see and have a thoroughly unhealthy lunch, on your father."

"And undo all the good done by our stay at the health farm," sighed Carol.

Ian tried to telephone Fifi to tell her that he would be coming home a day early, but he could never get any answer from Bryony. Eventually, he telephoned her parents' house in London, terrified that she might have fled to them with her story or, he thought, she might just have gone to town for a couple of days to frighten him. Martin, the butler, informed him that Lady Florence was not there, nor had she been there, and she was not expected.

Mystified, Ian flew into Heathrow and drove home. He could see the lights in the hall and on the stairs as he turned in the gate, and for a moment was pleased at the thought of the surprise in store for Fifi. It wasn't often that he returned from a trip earlier than planned, in fact he was usually later. It was when he opened the front door and was confronted with that odour peculiar to empty houses that a feeling of impending disaster crept over him. He realised then that the lights that were on were the automatic 'warning' lights that came on at dusk every day. Hopefully he called out, "Fifi?" but his voice echoed back to him.

He picked up the pile of mail on the hall table, glared at the 'post-it' note on the mirror, which informed him that Gladys had done the house and would be in Saturday morning as usual. Frowning, he went into the lounge and sat down on the chair by the telephone. Whom should he telephone to ask Fifi's where-abouts? It was a dilemma. Some of her friends were his ex-mistresses, they would gloat if she had left him. Her parents, whilst wanting to preserve the status quo, would certainly be very disapproving of him. Idly he opened the first envelope. It was an invitation to a dinner party, with "black tie", and "RSVP", engraved in the appropriate places. Did Fifi understand the position she would put him in if she vanished off the face of the planet? How was he supposed to explain her defection? He opened the second envelope.

It was from a London firm of solicitors, stating that they had been retained by Lady Florence Bannerss in the matter of her application for divorce. Would he please inform them which firm would be acting for him? Lady Florence had considered that he might think using Brian Martin, their usual solicitor, inappropriate under the circumstances. The words swam before Ian's eyes. He went cold at the thought of the "circumstances" being made available to Brian, his summer tennis partner, his drinking partner at The Bull. Fifi had not thought this thing through, she hadn't discussed it with him. He could think of a thousand reasons why things had happened as they had.

"I don't want a divorce," he protested aloud, and was immediately embarrassed by the sound of his own voice.

The children, he thought suddenly. Fifi would never go away without telling the children where she was. She had always been a very responsible mother.

Pulling the telephone onto his chair, he dialled Camilla's flat. She answered almost immediately.

"Hi."

"Camilla," he grumbled censoriously. "Your education cost a fortune and you still continue to talk in mid-Atlantic slang. What, if anything, is 'hi' supposed to mean?"

"It means 'hello' in shorthand. It sounds as if you've returned from Bermuda with a tan and a bad temper."

"I came home to find an empty house, and no word as to where your mother is. Have you spoken to her?"

"Yes, Tuesday, I think it was."

"Where is she?"

"In London."

"London is a big place. Could you be more specific?"

"I'm afraid I can't. I suppose she's at Granny's."

"I telephoned them from Bermuda, and from Miami, on Wednesday and Thursday. They had no idea where she was."

"Well, she'll bob up."

"In the meantime I'm on my own for the weekend. I kept it clear so that we could have a little time alone together to talk things over." He sounded bitterly aggrieved, then added, "Perhaps you'd come down and keep me company, look after me for a while."

"No way!" interrupted Camilla, "I'm just starting my two weeks holiday and I'm off to Kos tonight. We booked months ago. We've got to be at Gatwick by 11.30 and I can't wait. I'm going to lie in the sun, and swim, and drink for the whole two weeks."

"Couldn't you defer it for a month and come down here until this mess is sorted out?"

"Dad-dy! There are four of us going, and we've scrimped and saved for it. I've worked a whole year for this moment. Anyway, I hate the country as much as Mummy does. Gladys still comes in, doesn't she?"

"It's not the same thing. I can't talk to Gladys." Then he added prudishly, "I hope you don't go about on the beach topless."

Camilla giggled.

"No. I take care of my boobs. I wouldn't want them to get sunburned. But I wear thongs, so you might say I go bottomless instead, and I've got to go now, this minute. Kiss, kiss."

"Camilla?" he called, but she had hung up.

There was no doubt in his mind that she knew where Fifi was, and that she wasn't going to tell him. It was extraordinary how women stuck together.

He dialled William's digs in Exeter. It rang and rang. Out at the pub instead of working, thought Ian contemptuously, and was just about to hang up when the receiver was picked up at the other end.

"'Lo."

"William?"

"Oh, Dad. I was just listening to a concert. Wait a sec, while I turn it down."

Ian could hear the music in the background suddenly stop. William's voice sounded less muffled when he came back, as he boomed, "I have returned."

Ian grinned. William had obviously been asleep listening to the concert, and was now awake.

"Have you heard from your mother?" asked Ian, not intending to mince words. If women stuck together, so surely would men.

"About the divorce, you mean? Yes, she phoned me."

"Where from? Do you know where she is?"

"She's in London, isn't she?" asked William in a surprised voice.

"Yes, but where?"

"At Granny's, I presume."

"No, she isn't, and I have to talk to her. This whole thing has got out of hand. I flew back early so that we could have a sensible discussion. The last thing I want is a divorce."

"Unfortunately it can't always be what you do or don't want, Dad. Other people have desires and needs too."

"But it's over something so unimportant, so ridiculous. A floozy, a one-night stand, it could happen to anyone."

"Dad," interrupted William in a hard, very adult voice. "Remember me? I'm your son. I worked in your office as a gofer for three months, between A-levels and coming up here. During that time I was regaled with graphic descriptions of all your floozies, bimbos, secretaries, call girls, year-long affairs, and five minutes-over-desk flurries. It was all common knowledge. I even overheard some of your phone calls with reputed friends of Mummy's, so don't bother to put on an act for me."

Ian suddenly found it hard to breathe. Had he really been so careless, so indiscreet? Had the whole office been talking, and laughing, behind his back? He wanted to know, but couldn't bring himself to ask.

"I only ever loved your mother," he protested weakly.

"I love her too, that's why I'm sorry she's been exposed to this, besmirched by your licentiousness. Don't worry though,

I shan't volunteer any information. I don't approve of washing dirty family linen in public. I'm sure the whole case can be conducted discreetly."

"I do not want a divorce, discreet or otherwise, William. Tell your mother that. Try and dissuade her."

"That's not in my province. All I can do is advise her, in the best interests of the family name, to have a divorce on the grounds of marital breakdown due to your many absences, and avoid the vulgarity of infidelity."

Ian was furious, but kept his voice calm.

"Do you have any idea where she is?"

"No. You must be in a better position to know which friends she could trust, unless of course, there's another man waiting in the wings."

"I'm sure there isn't," snapped Ian, horrified. "Your mother is not that sort of woman. She's always been above suspicion. I'll be in touch later."

Fortunately he could not see William's satisfied smile as he slammed down the phone.

"Pompous little asshole," Ian shouted furiously, and hurled the phone across the room. "They don't care. I'm the only one who wants to keep this family together. But they can't stop me. I'll find her myself."

He stormed up to the bedroom to find her address book, and began to open her drawers, but Gladys had been there first. None of Fifi's personal possessions remained; only the faintest aura of her perfume lingered in the wardrobe. Ian flung himself down on the bed and tried to keep the tears from escaping from his eyes.

12

Following Gladys's example, Ian stuck a note on the bedroom door for her, stating simply: "Jet lagged. Sleeping. Do not disturb". Then he shut off the bedroom telephone and went to bed, and slept the clock round. It had been very depressing to arrive home and have no one to share his triumph with, no one to boast to about his new quarter million pound a year salary, no one to soothe, admire and applaud him, but fatigue had numbed him sufficiently to allow him to sleep.

The house was silent when he woke late on Saturday afternoon. He bathed, shaved and dressed, and got himself a meal from the freezer. He tried to interest himself in the television, but found it too appalling, and began to wander aimlessly about the house. It was unbearably empty. He went into William's room and found it tidier than he had ever seen it. It smelled of furniture polish and damp. He hesitated outside Camilla's room. She had always kept her door closed, and a small pottery plaque on the door read, "Keep out of my boudoir". Cautiously he opened the door. Here too the odour of polish was strong, but there was also a faint aroma of flowers. For a moment Ian thought that here, at least, Fifi had left a bit of herself, but then realised that the small upper casement window was slightly open, allowing the fragrance of the jasmine that covered the wall on that side of the house, to seep through.

Percy's room brought a catch to Ian's throat. Percy, the unplanned member of the family, who had taken them by surprise, had always filled Ian with a sense of wonder. He was totally unlike his siblings in looks, and character, and even here his room, clean, tidy and polished as it was, still smelled of him. Leaving the door open, as if hoping that the smell of Percy would keep him company in the empty house, Ian opened the door of the linen cupboard. The scent of violets gushed out. Instead of putting lavender balls in with her linen, Fifi was in the habit of putting an unwrapped bar of Yardley's April Violets soap on each shelf, insisting that keeping the soap in storage for a few months hardened it, and made it last longer, and that while sheets scented with lavender were invigorating, the scent of violets was relaxing.

Ian inhaled deeply. Gazing at the neat rows of sheets, towels and pillowcases, he remembered Fifi saying when they first saw the house, "What a lovely large linen closet. I think it's every woman's dream to have rows and rows of freshly ironed sheets and household things. I could stand and look at mine for hours," and he had laughed and replied, "Then don't count on me for company. I'm not a man to get enthusiastic over household 'things'."

Now he was. Now he wanted his house, and everything in it, to be exactly as it had always been. Familiar. Safe.

As the scent of violets pervaded him he was suddenly reminded of another Violet. An important one. Fifi's grandmother, known to the family as Greatgranny to differentiate her from Thea. But where Thea was a lightweight, a butterfly, Violet could be classed as a heavyweight, an eagle. She lived with a maid-companion in her small house near Burnham Beeches, and it suddenly occurred to Ian that Fifi might have taken refuge there. It would be peaceful and quiet, and Violet wasn't as likely to ask as many questions as Thea. Perhaps, because of Violet's great age – she must be in her eighties, he thought – Fifi would not have encumbered her with details, and so there was a possibility that he could still bring about a reconciliation without anyone else knowing. Burnham Beeches wasn't far. He could drop in on her tomorrow. Sunday was the day for families visiting families. He saw her usually at Christmas, when Guy and Thea had a Christmas house party, and he supposed Fifi saw her at other times, but he had never asked as he had not been interested. Suddenly he regretted his indifference. He would have to think of some reason for going over there, and it wouldn't be easy. Violet was an intelligent, well-educated woman, and by no means senile. She would recognise subterfuge. Her father had been a don at Cambridge with nothing but his brain to offer his children. Violet was the only one interested. She had inherited all his academic leaning. Eagerly, she had learnt Greek and Latin, Italian and French, ancient history and philosophy, but there were few openings for women in the professional fields of the day, so she had married well instead; Robert Granier, a baronet, a man with an income, and similar interests to her own. Violet did the done thing and produced a son, Adrian, whose brief life ended in the first year of the Second World War, and Dorothea, who had also married well – a wealthy widower, the Earl of Cheswick.

Violet had handed the children over to a nanny, and embarked on foreign travel with her husband. They had been present on many important excavations before Sir Robert was dispatched by a snake in Tunisia. Widowhood had not hindered her. She continued to go on archaeological digs, and give public lectures on the results. She wrote learned books on Easter Island and Linear B, and translated old Greek tomes. She was an authority on early Roman glass, Celtic runes, and French Renaissance history and art. Ian always admired her publicly, chiefly because everyone else admired her, and it pleased him to be related, if only by marriage, though secretly he found her subjects unreservedly boring. However, he was willing to suffer any amount of boredom if it meant finding Fifi and halting her mad rush towards divorce. How dared she discuss it with their children before discussing it with him! A divorce at this moment would probably damage his chances of a knighthood, which seemed a distinct possibility in the near future.

Whilst he did his unpacking, Ian debated the idea of offering Violet the perfume he had bought for Fifi, but dismissed it as too frivolous; the ruby-set heart-shaped locket he had also bought as a peace offering would hardly be suitable, and the only other object that would be was a book he had bought for himself, and was loth to part with. It had been in a display case in the lobby of his hotel in Hamilton, a beautifully preserved 167-year-old book. A history of the island and the five founding families. It contained wonderful illustrations of the flora and fauna, and the slave record of one of the big houses. A publishers' convention was taking place at the hotel and the book had been put there for their benefit. A few members of the board of Ian's own company had expressed interest in it and, determined on owning it himself, Ian had let the others go into dinner whilst he had located the owner and closed a deal before rejoining his party. It was not that he was particularly serious about book collecting, but he planned to have it displayed on his coffee table every time he entertained guests from the boardroom. Now he had to consider whether this wouldn't be the only entree into Violet Granier's house. It was the sort of thing she would appreciate and was rare enough to warrant a personal visit. He wondered dolefully if Fifi could appreciate the sacrifices he was willing to make to recoup her.

Violet opened the door herself, as tall, thin, upright and lively as ever.

She was genuinely surprised.

"Why, it's Ian! What a surprise! Come in, do."

He followed her in to the pretty, beflowered drawing room and handed her the book, unwrapped.

"I was in Bermuda on business and this caught my eye. I immediately thought of you. It's not only the history of the island itself, but of the purchases of slaves and their cost and treatment. I am sorry I didn't have time to wrap it, the customs had to see it because of its age and rarity."

He had wanted desperately to say "value", and tell her how much it had cost, but he managed to check the impulse.

"How very kind," she said, sitting down and skimming through the pages. "I shall have hours of pleasure out of it, oh!" she laughed suddenly and called, "Peggy! You must come and look at this wonderful book."

Her companion came in, dish towel in hand, and peered over her shoulder. She said "Good morning," politely to Ian, but

66

could not bring herself to meet his eye. She had heard the facts. He was an "adulterer", and she was ashamed for him.

"Look at that, Peggy, they even kept records of the characters of their slaves, and notes about unsuitable tribes. There's one here listed as a 'runaway', poor thing, what did they expect? Here's a little one of only four years – kitchen help. Oh thank you, Ian, it is a most generous gift, and here I am waffling on when I expect that all you want to know is whether Fifi was badly hurt."

"What?" he gasped. "Has Fifi had an accident?"

"Oh dear. Didn't you know? It was in all the papers."

Ian had whitened visibly under his tan.

"Are you all right?" she enquired. "Would you like some water?"

"No, nothing at all. Just tell me what happened."

He was thinking in horror that he had taken her car because it was much smaller and easier to park at the airport, knowing that his Turbo was too powerful for her, and that she hated driving it. He heard Violet's voice from a long way off.

"She was, mugged, I think was the word they used. Peggy," she called towards the kitchen, "could you look through the papers that are waiting for collection and pull out Wednesday's – or was it Tuesday's? Anyway, the one about Fifi, and bring it to Ian. You can read about it for yourself," she said, adding in a kindly tone, "but she wasn't badly hurt and she fought him off."

"Fifi did?" He couldn't believe his ears. Fifi didn't fight.

"Yes, wasn't that brave? None of us knows what we can do until there is an emergency. She was knocked about a bit, but he didn't get anything."

"Where is she? I must see her."

"I'm afraid no one has told me where she is. In some nursing home or other, I believe; but more to save her from the gutter press than for her injuries. I've been assured by Thea that she is all right, well, one can be sure of that, otherwise Camilla wouldn't have gone away."

"I don't think that's any criterion. I can't imagine anything keeping Camilla from her holiday," Ian said bitterly.

"That's where you are so wrong. Camilla is a very caring, responsible person. She comes to see me often."

"But she hasn't got a car," exclaimed Ian, as if there was no other mode of transport.

"No. But luckily that nice man she works for, Benjamin Bloomenthal, has been a fan of mine since I lectured at Bristol University. He says I decided him in his choice of careers, and he brings her down. Would you like to stay for lunch?" She changed the subject as Peggy returned with two newspapers, the *Independent* and the *Mail*.

Ian smiled, guessing who read which, and accepted gratefully.

"We have enough for one extra, haven't we, Peggy?"

Peggy simpered, "Of course we do." Violet invariably had extra people to meals, and Peggy was always prepared.

"I haven't met Camilla's boss," Ian said. He hardly thought such a meeting would have been profitable to him.

"Haven't you? You'd find him very interesting. He's teaching Camilla so much which, I fear, is why she cultivates him. She sees him as a short cut to the top. She's very ambitious and will have an important career."

"Can we be talking about the same Camilla? I always thought of her as someone marking time until she found a man rich enough to marry."

Violet laughed.

"Oh, no. You've got the wrong end of the stick. Certainly she does not have my contempt for money, but she has my academic aptitude, plus your business acumen. Those are not the qualities that bake bread and rock cradles. Given the opportunity, I would probably have been an old maid too. Camilla has the opportunity to make money, and be her own person. She was born at the right time."

Ian enjoyed the meal, a simple country rabbit pie, followed by gooseberry crumble. To his surprise, Violet had read the reports of his meeting, and was very knowledgeable about business.

"It isn't something I approve of," she told him, "but newspapers are so expensive nowadays that one has to read them from cover to cover. The trouble with living too long is that you remember when things were value for money. I can remember when newspapers were one penny, now they are ten shillings and no better for it."

They sat outside in the garden to have coffee. Ian nervously broached the subject that had really brought him over to visit.

"Have they told you that Fifi wants a divorce?"

"Yes, and why."

"Oh! But the thing is that I don't want a divorce at all. I can't imagine life without Fifi there."

Violet gave her little old lady cackle.

"You can't imagine life without Fifi there to shore it up? It sounded to me as if you were already having a pretty good life that excluded Fifi."

"I didn't exclude Fifi. She was my real life. Nothing else was serious. If I had thought that she would be hurt . . ."

"Oh, come now," Violet interjected.

"Well, if I had thought that she would ever find out."

"That is very different."

"I realise that now. I came back especially, a day early, so that we could have a long talk about it."

'What is there to talk about?"

"That a divorce would serve no purpose."

"You want things to continue as before?"

Ian's spirits rose. Perhaps Fifi had asked Violet to negotiate for her.

"Yes, that's exactly what I do want."

"To have your cake and eat it? And what does Fifi eat?" There was an uncomfortable silence.

"Do you remember that verse in Omar Khayyam, 'The moving finger writes; and, having writ, moves on; nor all your piety nor wit shall lure it back to cancel half a line, Nor all your tears wash out a word of it'? There is no going back, Ian."

"Not going back, perhaps, but if I could see Fifi, speak to her, I'm sure I could persuade her to give me another chance, to start again."

"After twenty years of perfidy? Poor Fifi, she always saw the world, and the people in it, through rose-coloured glasses, and now the glasses are shattered. How will she survive, I wonder?"

"I'll make it up to her," Ian promised grandly. Violet raised her rather untidy eyebrows.

"How? It's an interesting proposition. You can't undo anything. You can't ease her hurt, mend her pride, cancel her humiliation, even restore her faith in faithless friends. No, I am afraid, Ian, that you will have to face the fact that you have utterly destroyed your marriage. Now it's just a question of the cleanest, tidiest way to manage the divorce, and then you must get on with your life."

"I didn't think people of your age approved of divorce," Ian said rather crossly.

Violet smiled.

"You mean you hoped we didn't. When I was young, divorce wasn't possible. It carried a stigma. Now, if I disapprove of anything, it would probably be marriage, it rather stifles individuality, doesn't it?"

"It didn't stifle mine," he replied indignantly.

She gave him a rather triumphant smile and said, "Not yours, but what about Fifi's?"

He drove home cogitating on what he had learned. Violet knew a Camilla he had never suspected of existing. William had become a critical, slightly priggish young man without Ian even noticing it was happening. What of Percy? He mustn't lose Percy's support. He touched the newspapers on the seat beside him. And Fifi – a Fifi he didn't know – Fifi the elegant, Fifi the amenable, had walked out, and then proved herself capable of fighting her own battles. It made her more desirable, more intriguing, and more frightening.

13

Carol dropped Fifi and Percy off at the Boltons, refused an invitation to come in, but adjured Fifi to telephone her before she returned to the flat on Sunday night if she was nervous about entering the building alone, because Carol would make a point of being in and would meet her in the lobby; then she drove away to pick up the threads of her own life again.

Martin took Fifi's suitcase, and said to Percy, "If you bring your case up, Master Percy, you can see what has been put in your room for you."

"What?" demanded Percy, "And for God's sake drop the Master. I've outgrown it."

Martin smiled.

"I'm delighted to hear it. You had better go upstairs then."

As Percy bounded lightly past him, Martin turned to Fifi.

"Her ladyship would like a quiet word with you in the morning room, Milady. She is waiting now."

Thea was sitting very still, in a room full of shadows.

"How are you, darling?" she greeted Fifi. "Feeling better?"

"Yes, I am. Shall I turn on the light?' She did so without waiting for agreement, continuing brightly, 'The patient is going to live. Martin said you wanted a word."

She was shocked to see Thea looking so tired, and hoped it wasn't caused by worry over her.

Thea twisted her handkerchief round her fingers, then unwound it, then twisted it again and said crossly:

"I hate people who fidget, don't you?"

A feeling of apprehension crept over Fifi. Why was Thea procrastinating?

"What is it, Thea? You'd better tell me."

"Guy has had a minor stroke."

Fifi let out a gasp.

"How bad?"

"Quite good really, so they say. No paralysis. His face is contused on one side, and his eye hideously bloodshot. In fact, he looks awful."

Fifi put her hand up to her own cheek, from which the last sign of bruising was fading into a pale green smudge.

"I know how he feels," she said, and then the thought struck her that it might have been the attack on her that had precipitated his stroke. "It wasn't my fault, was it? Because of my being attacked?"

"Good heavens, no! It had nothing to do with you. The doctor has been warning him for years, but he won't give up smoking, and drinking, or stop gambling. He was asleep when it happened. It woke him. He said he felt a burning, tingling sensation in his face, and he thought his eye had fallen out." Thea shuddered. "He got up, put on all the lights, rang all the bells, and crashed around his room making an awful noise. When I first saw him I thought he had bumped into something, but when Dr. Bennett came, he knew at once what it was. He said this is a warning. Worse is to come if he doesn't take better care of himself."

"It's no good him telling you. Pa won't take any notice of you. He has to tell Pa."

"He did. In exactly those words. You can imagine the reaction. Guy laughed like mad, and intoned 'Worse is to come – the end of the world is nigh'. He laughs and cries very easily now, which is apparently what a stroke does. Dr Bennett suggested that we got a male nurse as Guy might become very irascible. I said he always had been, but someone's coming from an agency soon. He'll live in so I can sleep more easily. When you see Pa, don't mention the stroke, or sympathise, or look startled at his appearance. He thinks he's back to normal, but I'm afraid his eyesight may have been affected. By the way, we've bought a computer for Percy to play with. A house of sickness is hardly amusing for a sixteen-year-old."

72

"It's better than school, anyway."

"Well, Guy had read about this computer program in the *Sporting Life*, his only newspaper, and he believes that it will tell him which horses are dead certs and which aren't. He wants Percy to show him how to use it. I suppose Percy does know how they work?"

"Of course he does. The modern young find it as easy as reading a book. We gave Percy one for his last birthday, but not for conducting betting assignments. I suspect that Percy spends too much time on that already."

"He comes by it honestly," Thea smiled wearily. "That's all I wanted to tell you and, of course, to be sure that you've recovered. Ian telephoned here to know how you were, playing the worried husband, and asked when he could see you. He's very persistent. He even went to see Greatgranny."

"Oh, no!" exclaimed Fifi, "He didn't upset her, did he?"

"Upset her? Greatgranny? She had a lovely time teasing him, and he gave her a very valuable book."

"I didn't know he had a book, let alone a valuable one. I thought the only thing he ever read was company accounts, and his bank book, whilst doing illustrations for pornographic books."

"What? What are you saying, Fifi?"

"Nothing." Fifi had forgotten that only she and Carol and her solicitor knew of the photographs.

"Come on. Let's go and have tea with Guy. He's dying to see you. Just treat him as you usually do."

As they walked along the hall Fifi said anxiously, "You look terribly tired, Thea. Is it worse than you're letting on?"

"No, but troubles never come singly. First there was you, and now Guy." Then she added with a catch in her voice, "All these years I've thought I was staying for the sake of convenience. He's been annoying me all my life and then, when I thought I might lose him, it was unbearable. I sat with him after Dr Bennett left, and held his hand, and when I thought he was asleep I begged him, 'Please don't die, Guy, I love you' and he opened his bloodshot eye and said smugly, 'I always knew you'd come round one day.' I could have killed him!"

Fifi burst out laughing.

"Oh, Thea, do women ever win?"

Thea's suggestion that Guy had been dying to see Fifi was quickly dispatched as nonsense when they entered the study.

"Where's Percy?" yelled Guy, without any other greeting. "Where's the boy? He's got work to do on that computer thing."

"He's up there, playing with it now," Fifi told him.

"It's not to play with. He's got to come up with some winners. We need the money. They tell me the roof is leaking again at Cheswick."

"I shouldn't worry about that yet, Pa. It's going to be a dry summer," Fifi said soothingly.

"How d'you know? Got a direct line to God suddenly? It's all very well for you," he grumbled, calming down a bit. "It'll be William's worry, not yours."

"Well, it won't be yet awhile. He hasn't graduated yet."

"Then where is William? Someone told me he was coming."

"I told you." Thea patted his shoulder. "And he is coming, but it's a long drive. He'll be here for dinner."

"We haven't had tea yet, and I've got to talk to him. That interfering Miss Bossy Boots, Camilla, has been to Cheswick. She says it needs re-wiring. That'll cost a lot of money." His head sunk on his chest as he mumbled, "Where is it all to come from, that's what I'd like to know."

Fifi laughed.

"Camilla doesn't know anything about re-wiring."

"She knows a lot more than you think, mark my words," Guy said grimly.

"And the end of the world is nigh too, I suppose," Fifi suggested.

Guy looked pleased.

"You think they all talk a lot of rubbish too. I told them . . ." and he stopped suddenly, staring off into space. Fifi glanced over at Thea who shrugged her shoulders, and rang the bell.

74

"Shall we have tea?" she asked as if there had been no break in the conversation.

Percy was furious at being called down to tea.

"I was in the middle of a program," he protested.

"You're not supposed to be watching the box," Guy snapped. "You've got to teach me to use that computer thing."

"You cannot be serious!" Percy said in a fair imitation of John McEnroe, "and I wasn't watching TV. I was setting up the betting log for tomorrow."

"Good lad," Guy nodded his approval.

William arrived in the evening, very solicitous of Fifi, Guy and Thea, but the whole weekend felt unreal to Fifi. She found herself looking for double meanings in everything that was said, having nightmares that her father had died, and Percy had become the Earl, and she couldn't find William anywhere. The only person who enjoyed every minute of it was Percy, and Guy when he was awake, which wasn't often. They bet Guy's money on horses and then watched them lose on TV.

On Sunday afternoon, Percy was driven back to school and, after a light evening snack, Fifi prepared to return to Carol's flat. The very thought of it made her shake.

"Are you cold, Fifi?" Thea asked in surprise.

"No," Fifi answered honestly through trembling lips. "But I'm scared stiff at the thought of going back into that building. I'll get over it."

"Of course you will," Thea told her absentmindedly. "Just remember that lightening never strikes twice in the same place."

William laughed.

"And that's rubbish for a start. Come on, Mumsy. I'll run you back."

Gratefully, Fifi accepted.

"I feel stupid," she admitted. "Mothers are supposed to look after their children, not vice versa."

"Consider it a temporary aberration," suggested William. "Are you going to stay long at Carol's?"

"I don't know." Fifi felt ashamed at having imposed on Carol's time as long as she had. "I don't seem to be able to think further than whatever day it is. I'm living in limbo."

"It'll probably be easier once the wheels of the law begin to turn, and you can plan your future."

Fifi agreed that it would definitely be easier.

"But you are comfortable and happy in Carol's flat?"

"Apart from getting in," she laughed ruefully.

William took her up to the flat and opened the door for her, and yelled.

"Carol! Hi! Returned, one wandering mother."

Carol emerged from the bathroom wrapped in a towel.

"Sorry about this. It's hair-removing Sunday," she joked.

"Leave me with my illusions," protested William, "I thought women were born without hair."

"When did you grow that beard?" asked Carol. "You look quite dishy."

"I started it last year. With my round face no one took me seriously, so I grew this beard as a disguise. Now even the tutors doff their hats to me."

William was a masculine version of Thea. He had round, surprised blue eyes, a pink and white skin, short nose, and round face. Until he had grown the beard he had never looked more than twelve years old. Now at least he looked like an adult.

"I don't wonder. It's a great improvement. I almost fancy you myself. Would you like a drink, or some coffee?"

"No thanks. I'll get back. I've got to leave at the crack of dawn. Don't worry about Grandfather, Mumsy, he's a tough old bird."

"He didn't look very tough tonight." Fifi's voice cracked, and she was ashamed to find tears rolling down her cheeks. "Oh God, I'm sorry." She tried to brush them away. "I don't know why I'm doing this all the time."

"It's all right. It'll get better." William looked embarrassed.

Carol went and put her arm round Fifi, signalling to William with the other arm and mouthing, "Go on. She'll be all right . . ."

"Bye now." William made for the door. "I'll keep in touch."

"And so will Ian," grumbled Carol. "He telephoned just after six, having craftily worked out when Percy would have left to go back to Eton."

"How did he know I was staying here?" Fifi blew her nose.

"Someone had shown him a newspaper cutting about the mugging, and it said you were staying with me. I told him that you and Percy were at your parent's, and would be staying there a few days more. It seems he's managed to avoid admitting that you have left him. He said he didn't want you to speak to anyone else before you had spoken to him."

"I hope he won't bother Thea again. She has enough on her plate. Pa's had a small stroke."

"I shouldn't think that'll deter Ian. The best thing is for you to see the solicitor again and then he can contact Ian's solicitor and tell him this harassment must stop. We'll leave the Ansaphone on all the time to siphon off his calls, and he'll get fed up."

"Why can't he leave me alone? Hasn't he done enough to me?"

"Perhaps if you saw him and told him to his face that it was finished he . . ."

"I can't," wailed Fifi. "I love him. When I see him I still want him physically; it's so humiliating. He didn't lust after me unless there was no one else, but I think of him and go weak at the knees."

"Fifi, the world is full of bulls. When you think of him, put a bull's head on him and a ring through his nose."

"I'll try," she sniffed, "and I will go and see the solicitor. Maybe if he threatened Ian with a Court Order he'd stop trying to see me."

14

The return journey from Kos had not gone as smoothly as they had expected. They had had to hang about in Athens from midnight until 6 a.m. Then their plane had been diverted to Luton because of bad weather, which meant a train journey at a moment when the finances were so low they could hardly raise the price of a cup of filthy lukewarm coffee served in the buffet car. After the trip the flat seemed particularly welcoming.

"Home!" exclaimed Camilla, throwing her hold-all down and watching it slide across the wood floor. "Like which there is none other."

"Ah, yes. Undoubtedly home is where the heart is," agreed Daphne, the other female flatmate, adding, with a wheezy chuckle, "Not to mention dirt, dishes and poverty."

The two male members of the group still stood uncertainly in the doorway, giving each other meaningful, and encouraging glances. Finally Barney spoke up.

"We've been thinking, Camilla, that as you and I slept together on holiday, and Daphne slept with James, why don't we continue the arrangement? Instead of you two girls sharing, and James and I sharing, we could pair off as we did in Kos."

"No way, Jose," chorused the girls in unison. "That was just for the holiday."

"It wouldn't work permanently," explained Daphne.

"It was just a bit of fun. Nothing serious," put in Camilla. Barney's face registered shocked surprise.

"It was serious for me. You've always known how I felt about you, Camilla."

"Yes, but you know that we all agreed when we took the flat together that it would be strictly platonic, otherwise there would be endless complications. Holidays are different. That's sort of off duty so it doesn't matter."

"It matters to me, now," Barney said angrily. "I thought we were an item."

"We were, there. But we're here now, so we're just mates again. Be real, Barney, this is life, not the movies. Come on, Daphne, let's unpack."

The girls picked up their hold-alls and went into their bedroom, shutting the door firmly.

They each collapsed in a giggling fit on their respective beds.

"Imagine! One of them, forever," gasped Camilla.

"And their room smells," Daphne spluttered, at which moment the door burst open.

"What's so funny?" demanded an irate Barney. "Do you think it's funny to hurt people?"

James, pale and indignant beneath his tan, stood behind him.

"No, I don't," snorted Camilla, "And this is just what I meant about us not pairing off. This is the sort of silly row that would be going on all the time. I would never be able to have a private joke with Daphne because you're so conceited and egoistical you'd always think we were talking about you, and I couldn't take that twenty-four hours a day."

"Haven't you ever heard the saying that a man wrapped up in himself makes a very small parcel?" put in Daphne, and then swept past their glowering countenances towards the kitchen, saying, "I hope we've got something to eat."

Immediately there was a scramble behind her.

"The big tin of baked beans is mine," shouted James. "It's my reserve fund."

"I've got a tin of baked beans too," Daphne told him.

"Good," Camilla put the small bottle of red wine she'd taken from the plane onto the table, "and I've got an onion and a tin of frankfurter sausages. What have you got, Barney?"

Barney foraged through the fridge.

"I've got a little cheddar, and three slices of rather stiff bacon."

"Right. Then I'll make a paupers' cassoulet," announced Camilla. "Anyone like to slice the onion?"

Three heads shook in unison.

"It's lucky I'm not like the little red hen who wouldn't let anyone eat who hadn't helped," said Camilla, slicing the onion herself.

She emptied one tin of beans into the casserole dish, and laid the sliced onion on top. This was followed by the three slices of bacon, the frankfurters cut up, then the second tin of beans, the old cheese grated and the quarter litre of wine. The casserole was shoved into the oven and the door banged.

"Somebody ought to go out for a loaf of bread," hazarded Daphne.

There were no offers. The residents of the flat were getting back to normal.

"I'd better go," volunteered Camilla, "as I seem to be the only one not afraid of being mugged when out on my own."

Barney and James immediately proffered their services.

"Alright," Camilla bowed out gracefully, "if you insist. And if I give you the money can you get a bottle of plonk at the off licence?"

"Sure thing." Barney was looking on her with favour again.

"This is only a one-off,' she warned. "Tomorrow it's back to everyone paying their own whack again."

"Typical, isn't it?" proclaimed Daphne when they had gone. "If it's free and no effort they can be shamed into it, but if they have to work for it, they don't want to know."

She took four glasses from the cupboard and held them up to the light, inspecting the smears.

"Ugh!" She shuddered. "What we need here is a good wife."

"Everyone needs a good wife," said Camilla. "Actually, my mother will be coming vacant soon, but I wouldn't want to use her, she's been used too much already."

"By you?"

"No, Dad, of course. He always uses everyone 100 per cent.'

"I quite like my father."

"I used to adore mine, till I found him having it off on a pile of guests' coats on Mumsy's bed." Camilla smiled reminiscently. 'There was this great white moon wobbling around and the squealy voice of a friend of Mumsy saying, 'Oh, Ian. Oh, oh, Ian, oh,' and they must have seen my shadow and she said, 'Ian, there's someone there', and he said, 'Shut up and concentrate, or you'll miss it'." Camilla laughed aloud at the memory. "I rather hoped he'd shag himself to death. At thirteen you think your parents are too old for that sort of thing. I knew then that he was not adorable at all. I am not going to get married, it's a dead loss for a woman."

"I shall marry," Daphne stated, "just as soon as I can find someone rich enough so I will never have to work again."

"There's work, and work," Camilla said mysteriously. "Do you consider washing glasses work? Are you going to wash them, or just admire them?"

15

Benjamin Bloomenthal was delighted to have Camilla back at work. She had been with the firm for nearly two years, having started on a Fine Arts Course, after which she stayed on to train as a valuer, and she had made herself useful to everyone. Camilla was always the first to volunteer for overtime, willing to do secretarial work if needed. Her shorthand was efficient, and any typing she had to do was always handed in on time. She knew the history of a lot of the Heritage Houses they were called to estimate for, or arrange restoration work for, and she was keen to learn more. She borrowed books on silver markings, and porcelain designs and colours, to study at home in her spare time, and Bloomy, as he was called, was glad that she was attached to his department. He always predicted a great future for her if she didn't get married too soon.

Camilla had further enhanced her image by introducing him to her great-grandmother, Violet, Lady Granier, whom he had admired from afar for years, and who was an even greater authority on Georgian silver than he was. Camilla had taken him down to lunch with the lady, and she had graciously autographed a collection of her own books for him. As if all this was not enough, Camilla was also very pretty and he lusted after her, but in secret. He knew that, at forty-three, he was old by her standards, and Jewish, and she probably thought him dirt common as well, though she would undoubtedly be too well-bred to admit it, so Bloomy kept his admiration on a business level, but always managed to get Camilla included in any work he was undertaking. He excused the fact that it was Camilla he always asked for by saying that her efficiency and good taste were a great help, and this brought her some recognition among the other specialists; and she was politely grateful to Bloomy for this. As it happened, she admired his judgement and ability, and hoped to learn all he knew. Her admiration and devotion flattered him, and it did not occur to him that Camilla was grooming herself for his job.

As soon as Camilla returned from Kos, Bloomy took her down to Marsh House, where the firm were arranging an auction, a bankrupt estate sale. Some of the paintings and porcelain were expected to fetch high prices, but the furniture, the expert gloomily forecast, would be second-rate.

"Monastery oak trestles and Chippendale 'style' chairs," he complained in the car going down.

"Shall I make an note of that comment, Mr Street?" Camilla asked mischievously, but smiled so winningly that he had to smile back.

"You'll see I'm right," he predicted.

"How can you tell if you haven't even seen the outside of the house?"

"I don't know, Camilla, but after a time in this job you just get feelings."

"I hope I do," Camilla said honestly. A built-in Geiger counter for real or fake antiques would be a very useful talent.

After Camilla had watched Bloomy catalogue the Chinese bowls and vases, she wandered away, at his suggestion, to see if she could find something that he would consider valuable. To exercise her instincts, as he called it. She brought back an ivory Japanese netsuke.

"It could be a fake," she announced. "It isn't signed, but it looks like Raidin, the Thunder God."

"You have been doing your homework," Bloomy cried admiringly. "Not many people know to look for signatures on these little toggles."

"I learnt at a hard school," explained Camilla. "Grandfather has a whole collection of them at Cheswick Manor, and when they were in favour he was always explaining them to me."

"Your grandfather is the Earl of Cheswick?" demanded Bloomy, trying to keep the awe out of his voice.

"Yes, he is," she answered offhandedly, "and he keeps about forty-five of these in his bedroom. Are they valuable?"

"Valuable! A signed netsuke can cost as much as £30,000. And he keeps them in his bedroom?"

"Yes. He keeps all his toys there." Camilla had to laugh at his bewildered expression. "I know what you're thinking – the aristocracy are eccentric."

"No, no," he protested.

"Now, come on, Mr Bloomenthal, that's exactly what you were thinking, though probably in different words. You were saying to yourself, 'nutcases', all of them, and you're probably right. Grandfather had a habit of starting a collection, and then getting bored with it. It disappears into a cupboard in his room, and then he starts collecting something else. Before the netsuke he collected silver snuff boxes, and after the netsuke he collected sovereign cases completely full of gold sovereigns. I loved playing with them when I was little." She gazed wistfully into space as if trying to recapture that little island of childhood. "But best of all I loved his Chinese bottles with the tiny spoons attached to the lids, and the pretty paintings in the glass."

Bloomy sighed.

"I would love to see Cheswick Manor, and all its wonderful treasures. I suppose Sotheby's did the inventory for CTT?"

"It was a long time ago. I'm not absolutely sure, but I believe they did. But none of Grandfather's personal 'toys' were included. He never considered them worth insuring so . . ."

"What?" shouted Bloomy, and then clapped his hands over his mouth and looked nervously round to make sure no one had noticed.

"Well, he just considers them his playthings, little pleasures. I don't think he's even had his collection of French toy soldiers and Napoleonic battles insured. He thinks they're quite safe in the night nursery. No one ever goes in there."

Bloomy sighed again. He loved rare things, old things, beautiful things. It seemed terrible when they were wasted on the wealthy who just "played" with them.

"Oh, how I would dearly love to see some of these exquisite treasures that you speak of so casually," he said longingly.

"Would you really?" asked Camilla innocently, knowing full well that he would.

He nodded, too hopeful to speak.

"I'll arrange it," she said grandly. "Why don't you drive me down on Sunday afternoon? I'll show you round."

"That would be wonderful. Can I take you to lunch first?"

"I'd enjoy that," she accepted graciously.

Bloomy couldn't believe his luck.

Between then and Sunday, Camilla had some cards printed which read, 'Camilla Bannerss. Assistant to B Bloomenthal'. She knew now that it was only a matter of time.

They lunched at the Compleat Angler at Marlow. As they left he asked if her grandfather had given permission for him to tour the house.

"No need," Camilla answered loftily. "I'm allowed to go there any time I like. It's our second home really. I telephoned and told the caretaker and housekeeper that you and I are supposed to make notes of all the repairs that need doing. They'll be delighted to see us. They keep writing to the Estate Manager, and he keeps writing to Grandfather, about the roof leaking, and the ancient electric wiring catching fire, but Grandfather just ignores it. He says the Estate Manager is so busy boozing with the farmers that he doesn't know what's going on. Of course, there's no money for renovations anyway."

"If the Earl's small collections are as fine as you suggest, he could sell them. That would pay for a portion of the roof, and some re-wiring."

Camilla laughed.

"You know as well as I do that after he's paid auction room fees, our commission and tax and profits tax, there wouldn't be enough left to buy a bucket to put under the smallest hole in the roof to catch the rain, let alone re-tile it."

"Ah, but you did say," responded Bloomy, looking enormously pleased with himself, "that there is no record of the 'toys'."

"There isn't, but there would be a record of the sale."

"Not necessarily. Small collections can leave the country privately, to go to collectors in France or Italy, Sweden or Switzerland, those are good private markets."

Camilla held her breath, though she wanted to whoop with delight. Bloomy was about to take her into the inner circle, the secret track of the art trade.

"Isn't it against the law?" she asked breathlessly, opening her eyes wide in simulated awe.

"Of course not. I never do anything against the law," Bloomy said grandly. "Dealing with private collectors in this manner is standard business practice. It is done quite openly."

"Really? Oh, I have so much to learn, haven't I?"

"But then, you learn so quickly. You see, if, for instance, your grandfather decided to sell a small, portable collection, the agent, you or I or whoever it might be, would contact known collectors of similar items in other European countries. There would be a brief auction by letter and, when the price was arrived at, the agent would take the collection over."

"And get caught at the airport as the silver bleeped madly going through the security screening."

Bloomy laughed.

"It's not quite as primitive as that." Seeing her rapt expression, and enjoying her admiration for his superior knowledge and experience, he threw all caution to the wind. "One drives to Dover or Folkestone to pop over for a romantic lunch in France. A day trip on the ferry is considered to be quite a fun thing, I believe. The purchaser's agent meets one in Boulogne, or Calais, at some small, well chosen restaurant. Afterwards the purchasing agent takes the collection and hands over the money, which goes into the bottom of a carrier bag with wine and cheese on top to cover it up, and we come home."

"With cash?"

"Of course. Cheques can be traced, cash can't. Then, if you are still talking of your grandfather, I would take my commission, already agreed upon, and give you yours, and the Earl would have the rest. Tax free."

"Like prostitution?" giggled Camilla. "Oh, it's all so cloak and dagger, I've gone all shivery."

Smiling, Bloomy said, "There's nothing to it."

Camilla shook her head.

"I don't know if I'd dare. I'm a dreadful coward, and I always feel guilty coming through customs."

"I'm sure you look the picture of innocence," Bloomy assured her.

Barker admitted them without any questions, but begged her to pay particular attention to the roof over the nursery wing. It was leaking so badly that he had had to go up in the attic himself and spread out some plastic sheeting.

"Thank you, Barker. That's just the sort of thing we need to check. Then I'll tell Granny and she'll arrange it. Grandfather isn't well."

"I'm sorry to hear it, Miss. Will you and the gentleman be here for tea – ?"

"Yes please, about 4.30. And if Mrs Barker has some of her 'cut and come again' marmalade cake, we wouldn't say no."

Barker smiled and left them.

"Now come on," she said to Bloomy, "We'll start upstairs and work down."

Businesslike, she took out her note book as she spoke.

Bloomy needed no urging. For two hours he peered at paintings, lifted vases, turned back rugs to inspect the weaving underneath. He frowned at the spreading damp on the nursery ceiling, and told Camilla that the antique teddy bears, dolls and clockwork toys should be removed to a place of safety at once, as some of them were priceless. When he saw the soldiers in their campaign positions in the night nursery, he almost wept.

"Suppose the ceiling caves in on them," he moaned. "Even if they were insured they couldn't be replaced."

Worse confronted him in the Earl's bedroom. Whilst he examined the netsuke in silent joy, Camilla found signs of a fire on the carpet, and round the electrical plug on the wall. When she pointed it out, Bloomy's only thought was to take the collections to a place of safety.

"We can't do that," Camilla protested. "I haven't the authority. But I'll mention it to Barker."

After examining everything, Bloomy told her that he could guarantee that the Earl would have enough money to mend his roof if he sold the netsuke only, and that he, personally, knew a suitable buyer. Camilla spent a pleasurable few minutes trying to guess what her share of the commission would be.

She did not need money, but she liked the idea of having a lot in her bank account to admire. Money is power, she thought to herself.

They had tea and promised Barker that help would be forthcoming, then Camilla mentioned the burns.

"Yes, Miss," Barker said solemnly. "We have had two or three small fires, caused by short circuits. I'm afraid the rain gets into the attic and some of the wires become damp and then it's a short circuit. Mr Harvey did get an electrician up, but he said the whole place had to be re-wired."

"You and Mrs Barker might be burned to death in your beds!" exclaimed Camilla indignantly.

Barker smiled.

"They are only little fires, Miss," he replied.

"The house might burn down. Oh, poor William, and he's so looking forward to living here."

"Who is William?" Bloomy asked, jealousy creeping over him.

"William is my elder brother. He's going to inherit this crumbling pile." Camilla giggled. "I never realised before why people referred to Cheswick as a crumbling pile, but it's very apt."

Before they left, Bloomy disappeared into the downstairs loo. When he came out he was white-faced.

"I think those are original Rowlandsons in there. Do you have any idea what valuation they put on them for CTT?"

"You don't value things in the lavatory," laughed Camilla. "I think those pictures are vulgar, that's why they're in that lavatory. It's for gentlemen. We have two pretty Marie Laurencins in the ladies."

"Not valued either?"

"Of course not. You can't invite insurance men into the loo."

Bloomy was exasperated. People who had always had money didn't seem to understand the value of their possessions.

"Getting paintings abroad takes a little more planning," he said thoughtfully as they drove back to London.

"But it could be done if it was worth it?" Camilla asked.

"It would be worth it."

"Then I think we've got a deal. I'll speak to Granny."

"Don't mention it to anyone else," advised Bloomy. "The fewer people who know about it the better."

"Even though it's quite legal," Camilla teased.

"It's not the legality we must worry about, it's the attitude of our firm towards moonlighting."

"Say no more," agreed Camilla. 'I'll get a zip for my lip. This will be our secret."

16

An office is not the ideal place to hear the announcement of your impending divorce. To Ian it was the final straw. He had the impression that he was no longer in control of his life. From the moment that Fifi had left the marital home, he had been convinced that she was being advised and manipulated by his enemies. A powerful, wealthy man, he thought, always had enemies anxious to topple him, but he had not expected the attack to come from that quarter, his most vulnerable and previously reliable ally, Fifi.

That the fault lay with him did not occur to him. Until this actual morning he had managed to keep all information about his personal problems to himself with the exception of Geoffrey, in whom he had confided in exchange for the name of a first-rate solicitor, because, even though he was going to prevent the divorce if he could, he wanted to keep his back covered. The solicitor Geoffrey recommended had handled his divorce case and managed to achieve a financial settlement within reasonable, some even said miserly, bounds. That Nicola had won in the end was her personal achievement, and not due to any laxity on the solicitor's part. Nicola had merely said that the yearly income made it impossible for her to keep the house and, rather than buy a smaller one in the same district, she would take the boys and go and live with her mother outside Inverness. It meant that Geoffrey was only able to see the boys on very rare occasions, but that could not be blamed on the solicitor, and he had enabled Geoffrey to keep the better part of his fortune to spend on Marge. Ian felt that this was the sort of solicitor who might know how he could keep his marriage together and, if not, would see to it that Fifi had to fight for everything she got.

So, when Ross poked his head round the door and said, "Kelly and I were so sad to hear about you and Fifi, Ian. You were the couple we were aiming at becoming. If there's anything we can do, just shout; meals, a shoulder to cry on, all that sort of thing," Ian's immediate reaction was that Geoffrey had blabbed.

"Geoffrey couldn't keep his big mouth shut, I suppose," he said disgustedly.

Ross looked surprised.

"Geoffrey? I haven't seen him this morning, but I guess everyone else saw it in the paper too."

Ian suppressed a gasp and tried to sound jocular.

"Not in the headlines, I hope."

Boy! thought Ross admiringly, these stiff-upper-lip Englishmen never lose their cool, and he smiled and answered, "No, sorry. Headlines are reserved for film stars and Royalty, in that order. You have to make do with the 'dish the dirt' page."

As soon as he had retreated, Ian sent for a selection of the morning papers. Fifi read the *Telegraph*, and sometimes the *Mail*, so he looked through those first. It was time-consuming but he didn't want to ask any of the staff to do it. He found it hard to believe that Fifi had given out an announcement to the papers without a word to him. It was most un-Fifi-like behaviour, but then, that was how Fifi was behaving at the moment.

He found the offending item on the gossip page under the heading Trouble Shooter Shot. It read:

'Ian Bannerss, who has just smoothed the path for the MTM takeover of RFT Amalgamated, is finding his own personal path anything but smooth. Lady Florence Bannerss had admitted to one of our correspondents that they have separated, and that she is seeking a divorce. There are three children of the marriage. The eldest, William, is heir by special remainder to the Earl of Cheswick, the father of Lady Florence. The Earl, who has recently suffered a minor stroke, is rumoured to want his grandson to take the family name of LeRoser by deedpoll.'

"He'd better not," shouted Ian to his empty office. That would be tantamount to William repudiating him. "He'd damn well better not!"

It was at this inconvenient moment that Mr Cross of Cross, Baron and Cross, telephoned to say that he had had a communication from Lady Florence Bannerss's solicitor, requesting an undertaking for Mr Bannerss to refrain from either telephoning or trying to see Lady Florence. Failure to comply with the request might lead to an application for an injunction.

That did it. Ian was a fighter, he liked a challenge. Shouting to his surprised secretary to cancel all his appointments, he stormed from the office.

He took a taxi to New Cavendish Street, and minutes later was ringing the doorbell of Carol's flat.

Unsuspecting, Fifi opened the door. When she saw Ian standing there, she was too startled to say anything and after that first second couldn't think of anything to say.

Realising at once that he had gained an advantage, Ian said, "Hello, Fifi. May I come in?"

"Of course," she answered through dry lips, and stood aside. "I don't know if we're supposed to, to . . ."

"To see each other?" he finished for her. "Supposed by whom?"

He walked past her into the living room. Although he had never liked Carol, she had been an old school friend of Fifi's, and they had visited quite often and he knew his way around the flat. He sank down into a deep armchair and Fifi perched on the very edge of an upright chair. Used to reading reactions and attitudes during business meetings, Ian made a mental note, "ready to bolt for it". It caused him some amusement, and boosted his confidence.

"Solicitors, I suppose," she admitted weakly. "I don't know much about divorce, never having done it before."

As she sat close to the window, the sun sent shafts of golden light through her hair which, Ian noticed, she had had cut very short. Had the mugger hit her on the head? He couldn't remember if anyone had mentioned it. She had also lost a good deal of weight, and looked very fragile sitting there. He felt a sudden wave of tenderness for her.

"And you're not going to do it now," he said seriously. "Look what it's doing to you, Fifi. You're fading away. No one in their right mind throws away a lifetime of shared memories on a whim."

"I haven't," Fifi interrupted quickly, knowing that his "logical" arguments always left her the loser.

He sat there, calm, unchanged. Handsome, clean, self-assured, perfectly dressed. No wonder I couldn't keep him, Fifi thought helplessly, and longed to weep, and throw herself into his arms, and be comforted.

"I don't know what idiot is advising you, Fifi," he continued, "but I know from the newspaper announcement this morning that they are not our kind of people."

Two frown lines creased on her forehead, and two deep furrows appeared above her nose, as they always did when she was puzzled. His heart contracted at the familiarity of it as she asked, "What announcement?"

"Haven't you seen the morning paper? If they didn't get it from you I can't imagine who is handing out such personal information. Carol? I hate to think how the children will react."

"Which paper? What does it say? Carol left the paper in her room, I'll go and get it."

Flustered, she hurried out and returned with the paper. From force of habit she handed it to him to show her where the article was, and he did.

"But I never spoke to anyone. And that bit about Pa, yes, he is ill, so he definitely would not have been discussing anything like that with anyone, and he would have spoken to you before William. You know what a stickler he is."

"Unfortunately people bent on making trouble have little interest in the truth. Personally I should be extremely hurt if William abandoned his name."

"But he wouldn't," protested Fifi.

Ian smiled at her, stretched his long sexy legs out and said smoothly,

"Don't get upset yet, Fifi. This is only the beginning. In a case like this people will try to make things as unpleasant as they can."

"But why? It has nothing to do with anyone else, and certainly not the papers. We're not famous."

He shrugged and, as if they were in their home, asked, "Any chance of a cup of coffee?"

Habit again made Fifi jump to her feet.

"Yes, of course. I'll get some."

Minutes later she brought the tray in and put it on the coffee table, moving the newspaper aside as if it were dirty. Ian felt more confident than ever. Things were feeling more normal. She was pouring his coffee, speaking calmly to him.

"You shot off without even giving yourself time to weight up the pro's and cons of the situation," he began.

"There aren't any pro's, Ian." Suddenly Fifi had remembered what this was all about. Not a pleasant visit, a quiet chat over coffee with one's husband, but an unfaithful husband trying to – what? It was hard to fathom. She managed to continue steadily.

"How could there be? Apparently you were continually un-faithful, even with my friends, on your own doorstep for all I know, or in the house. You didn't need me, or respect me. The children are no longer children, so there is no reason to continue living what was obviously a farce."

He leant towards her, his elbows on his knees.

"We got on well together, didn't we? My affairs never interfered with out lives. They weren't serious, just a bit of fun. All men stray once in a while. The point is, Fifi, that our marriage was the one ideal thing in my life. To me it was perfect. It was good for you, too. You were always well and happy. It was an agreeable, comfortable arrangement. You were admired and I was very proud of you. There is no reason why things couldn't continue as they were. My infidelities didn't

94

make you unhappy before, so why should they now?"

"I didn't know about them before," Fifi argued stiffly.

"Well, now you do, and you can see that they meant nothing."

"Would it have meant nothing if I had been unfaithful?"

He was silent for a minute, twisting his cup round and round in the saucer, toying with the idea of being honest.

"No, but only because you are the person you are, and I know that the physical act for you is an act of love, whereas for me," he gave a little shrug, "it's a reflex action, which I will try and control in the future."

"Until the next time." She gave a wry smile.

"Perhaps, but I am getting older, time may be on your side."

Fifi desperately wished she could turn back the clock, wished that she could be as loving towards him as she always had been, but superimposed on the elegantly dressed man opposite her was the naked satyr she had seen in the pictures from his private drawer. A lump of ice seemed to press tightly against her chest, and tears pricked behind her eyes, but speaking carefully she said,

"I'm afraid we are both too old to change, and too old to surrender our ethics. I am sorry that word of the divorce got into the papers and caused you embarrassment. It was bound to become known sooner or later anyway, so perhaps it's all for the best."

"Doesn't our marriage mean anything to you? It does to me."

Suddenly a spark of anger was ignited in Fifi. She answered him through clenched teeth.

"Do you realise, Ian, that you have been speaking of marriage as if it was some inanimate object? You've said that you don't want to lose The Marriage, that The Marriage is important to you, but you've never once said, I don't want to lose you, Fifi, you are important to me. If it's just a marriage you want you can have it with anyone."

"Not this marriage. I have expended a lot of time, money and energy on this marriage and of course I want you, Fifi, that goes without saying. You make the marriage."

95

She ran her hands through her short curly hair and shook her head, trying to shake off the image his words evoked, but she knew now that he only wanted her because she had brought a title, position, good connections to the marriage. She was respectable and respected, and a lot of rumours that circulated around Ian were discounted because of her respectability.

"I'm sorry, Ian. It's no longer possible. I want a divorce."

His jaw squared, his eyes took on that familiar flint-like quality.

"I'm sorry too, because I can guarantee that you won't get one."

Her head snapped back with shock.

"Yes, that may surprise you, but I, too, have a solicitor. He assures me that as you have had intercourse with me after each of my infidelities, you have, in law, condoned them."

"I didn't know about them," gasped Fifi unbelievingly.

"That's just your word against mine. I shall insist that I confessed to you each time, with details, and you forgave me."

"You will be on oath." The rage in Fifi was gaining momentum.

"On oath or anything else. My dear Fifi, I am not afraid of God striking me dead over some piffling little lie in a divorce court."

Fury gave her strength.

"The choice is yours, Ian. You may do what you like. You can have the polite conventional marriage-breakdown sort of divorce that William favours, or you can have a filthy, hard-fought tabloid-headline one. Before you decide, you should consider who will be involved. People like Geoffrey. He might react badly when Marge is cited, and Brian might feel you were unworthy of his friendship when Janice is called. I have evidence of many others, mostly married, and some young enough to be your daughter."

"I see!" His voice was icy. "You certainly have changed. You don't care whose life you ruin to get your own selfish way. Well, it won't work, Fifi. I shall still insist that you condoned it. Relished it, in fact."

96

"Will you also say I admired all the nude photos of you with various women on your knee? Will *they* be happy to see themselves spread across the pages of the Sunday press? Will you persuade a judge that I didn't object to all the weekends at the Grand Hotels with other women using my name? That I was happy about the £500 pay-offs to call girls and ex-mistresses?"

Ian had also risen. He had forgotten the pictures, the receipts, and cheque stubs. He had searched Fifi's drawers but had never suspected that she might have searched his. He was shocked, not only at his own carelessness, but at her duplicity. Grim-faced, he tried a final attack.

"And I always respected you for the moral example you set the children, the love I thought you lavished on them. Now I see it was all a con. No mother who loved her children would involve them in the sort of media filth you are threatening."

A red haze descended over Fifi's eyes. Without thinking she reached for the cut glass vase of flowers on the table beside her and threw it.

"You fucking bastard!" she yelled. "You crud! You arsehole!" and with each word some article followed the vase. An ashtray, then an alabaster cigarette box and two books. "You shit! You dickhead!"

"Fifi!" protested Ian. "Fifi!" With his hands protecting his head he backed towards the door. "Calm down, Fifi!"

"Get out, you son of a bitch. You syphilitic cock!" she screamed, hurling an exquisite crystal music box at him.

A potted plant crashed against the door before he reached it and a large pottery ashtray fell just short of his feet.

"Fifi!" he gasped despairingly as a silver-framed, signed picture of Rex Harrison caught the side of his head. He couldn't believe that this virago was his serene and gentle wife. Neither could Fifi. She heard herself yelling things she didn't know she knew, throwing things and screaming in a totally alien manner. She was doing the unthinkable, making a scene, and she couldn't stop. Ian retreated through the living room door as his coffee cup and saucer caught him on the shoulder. Fifi advanced with the tray and coffee pot. He managed to get out of the front door without even stopping to straighten his tie or mop the coffee dregs from his jacket, and headed hurriedly for the lift.

Fifi stood for a moment staring into space. Then she started to laugh, shakily at first, and then more heartily. The situation had been ridiculous. People yelled and threw things when they were first married, not when the marriage was ending. She had never done it before. She had been too controlled, too inhibited. Perhaps throwing things was what he wanted, maybe it would have helped, but she had always been so anxious for his approval, for him to be pleased and happy. It was too late now, but she felt a wonderful sense of relief. The pain of the separation was gone. It was as if she had had a boil inside that had suddenly burst, letting the poison out. She looked with dismay at the broken glass, the coffee stains on the wall, the water on the carpet and the general mess.

Clearing up, Fifi found to her horror that the pottery ashtray she had thrown was the one made for Carol by her son, Jason. It was her treasure, an untidy copy of a blue and yellow one from Portugal. The break was almost clean, only a few coloured chips were missing. When the living room was almost back to normal, Fifi went out and bought paints, paintbrushes and fine surface polyfilla. This was something Fifi could do well. She had spent two summer holidays at archaeological digs with her grandmother, and she had learned to piece things together. At sixteen she had been set to work at a small antique shop near her grandmother's house where she had been spending yet another holiday. The job was to give her experience, pocket money, and prevent her from being bored. She had repaired, restored and artificially aged some of the stock.

When Carol returned, the ashtray was drying on the table looking as it always had, and Fifi felt better than she had in a very long time.

Fifi recounted the events of the morning and promised to replace everything.

"The breakages were in a good cause," Carol assured her. "I just wish I'd been here to see it."

"I'm glad you weren't. I'm so ashamed. Not of throwing them at Ian, he deserved it, but of breaking things that belonged to you. And oh, I wish I'd had a different upbringing. I couldn't think of enough names to call him."

17

The house in the Boltons had always been treated as a family house. Guy and Thea had always impressed upon Fifi that it was still her home, and home to her children, who came and went as they pleased, their bedrooms always ready for them, even if Thea and Guy were not in residence, so it was with some foreboding that Fifi received Thea's invitation for dinner that Saturday night.

"Isn't this a little formal?" she asked in alarm. "What's the occasion?"

"You'll have to ask Camilla, it's on her behalf that I'm inviting you. She has specified your presence, and William's, and stipulated that you are to be here by 6 p.m., so that we have time to talk privately before Guy joins us."

Fifi had lunch with Camilla the previous day and she had not mentioned it.

"Didn't she give you a hint?" Fifi asked hopefully.

"No, she was very mysterious. She just said it was urgent."

"Oh, God! I hope she isn't pregnant."

Thea laughed.

"She would hardly want William here to discuss that."

"True. Well, we'll just have to wait and see."

Camilla arrived straight from a country auction, wearing jeans and a T-shirt.

Thea threw up her hands in horror.

"Darling! You do look a scruff. Your grandfather will frown."

"I am a scruff, and he can frown as much as he likes. These are my working clothes."

William arrived a few minutes later, similarly clad.

"And are those your working clothes too, William?" Thea asked sarcastically.

"They're my only clothes," William replied.

"Don't worry, Thea, they'll outgrow it," Fifi comforted her. "It's the result of wearing uniforms at school. They grumbled about it all the time, but then found they couldn't break the habit. This is the uniform everyone wears at the moment."

"But there are such pretty frocks in the shops," sighed Thea.

Once they were all settled in their various favourite positions, Thea said:

"Out with it Camilla. We're dying of curiosity. Are you announcing your engagement?"

"How old fashioned! Nobody does that any more, Granny. I've no time for that sort of rubbish, and no one in mind at the moment."

"I'm very glad to hear it," Thea replied. "Greatgranny tells me that you've taken the same young man to see her three times. A nice young man, but Jewish."

"So was Jesus," Camilla snapped, "and Bloomy is hardly a young man. He must be over forty, and as romantic as an old boot."

"Well, that settles his hash then," William chortled, "and yours, Granny. I'm ashamed of you. I never thought of you as a bigot."

"I am not a bigot," protested Thea, "though I may be slightly prejudiced."

"You can't get away with that one. Prejudice is when you know something about someone that turns you against them, bigotry is when you're against them for no reason."

"I don't need a lesson in English from you, thank you, William." Thea wore her most disapproving expression. She did not enjoy criticism. Then she added, "All I can say is, how odd of God to chose the Jews."

"But odder still are those who choose a Jewish God, yet scorn the Jews," William finished for her.

"If you two have finished airing your views, I think we should get down to business," Camilla announced firmly.

William gave her a big grin.

"Have we a quorum, Mr President?" he quipped.

"Shut up," Camilla squelched him. "What I have to suggest is particularly important to you. I have been down to Cheswick twice recently. It's in a deplorable state. There have been at least two fires caused by old, faulty wiring; the roof is leaking badly; and the plumbing is antique, even if not dangerous. Something has to be done about it."

"We can't afford to do anything," protested Thea. "Your grandfather has let his finances get into an awful mess."

"I know," interrupted Camilla. "Percy told me."

"How did Percy know?" Fifi asked, breaking her silence.

"Grandfather told him ages ago. Anyway, that's why I thought we should have this conference. It's no good burying our heads in the sand, and hoping the old house will repair itself whilst we're not looking. It may help that grandfather has a collection of netsuke worth over a hundred thousand pounds."

There was a loud collective gasp.

"And," she continued, "there is a buyer for it. In Geneva."

"But we'd have to get it there, and by the time we paid dealers and taxes there wouldn't be . . ." interrupted William.

"Could you belt up for a minute?" Camilla said. "Grandfather's little collections are not listed officially as possessions of the estate. He collected them all so long ago, and never bothered to insure them, so . . ."

And she told them of Bloomy's suggestions.

"Is it legal?" was William's first worry.

"Apparently. In any case it is common practice."

"And what does whatever-his-name get out of it?" asked Thea.

"Twelve per cent of the purchase price, out of which he pays all travelling expenses, and my one per cent. It'll certainly leave you with enough to start re-roofing and re-wiring before the old place falls apart. There's a buyer waiting for the netsuke now, cash in hand. You could have it in ten days."

"It's very tempting," admitted Thea.

"Wow!" exclaimed William. "Have you worked out one per cent of £100,000?"

"Of course I have," Camilla said witheringly, "and that's only the tip of the iceberg."

"No wonder you never played with dolls," sighed Fifi. "They weren't interested in getting rich."

"Talking of dolls," began Camilla again. "The ceiling in the nursery is threatening to fall in with the weight of the water from the attic and there are some teddy bears, dolls and other toys there that are worth some money. Bloomy isn't in that line, but he thought you could get a few thousand. If you sold them all, it would pay for Grandfather's nurse. There is a toy sale coming up at Phillips soon. I could put them in for you, if you like."

"I'm sure it would be a big help," said Thea. "The staff are always asking me for money, and nobody else seems to be organising it."

This, thought Camilla, is going to be easier than I had hoped.

"There is a curator of an American military museum over on a scouting buying trip now. Bloomy has told him about Grandfather's collection of French regiments, and he's interested in the whole collection as it stands, with the guns and the tents, etcetera. How do you feel about that? That should bring in about £60,000 or more."

"I haven't seen these soldiers, have I?" queried William. "Perhaps I should look at them before they become a one per cent statistic."

"You ought to be grateful to me, William. I'm saving your inheritance for you and you *have* seen them. It's all those military campaigns set out in the night nursery."

"Oh, those." William dismissed them with a wave of his hand. "Toy soldiers."

"So, what do you think?" Camilla looked hopefully at Thea.

"I think you are definitely your father's daughter," said Fifi.

"Was there ever any reason to doubt it?"

"No, of course not," Fifi blushed furiously. "I just meant that you had inherited his better talents."

"I know, Mumsy. I was only teasing you. I forgot you hadn't any sense of humour."

"Your parentage is not something to joke about, Camilla," Thea said severely. "How do we go about arranging all this?"

"You don't have to do anything. No one will know from whence they came. Just give me a letter of authority to fetch the things from the nursery tomorrow. Bloomy will take me and the American to see the armies. If he wants them we'll fix the deal then and there, and ferret them out without Barker seeing. It will take time but we'll go down early. Grandfather also has a collection of snuff boxes, and about twenty-two silver vinaigrettes and about twenty-seven sovereign cases, the ones gentlemen used to carry in their pockets. These, if I remember rightly, had sovereigns in them." Camilla hardly had to remember at all as she had inspected all these things with Bloomy, but did not consider it necessary to mention that. "None of these are insured, or on the CTT list, so I could bring those back too and we could find buyers abroad, and you could have the money."

"It sounds dodgy to me," said William. "Too easy really, and not very honest."

"Oh, honestly, William! Look at it this way. If we manage to rescue Cheswick Manor, we are saving part of the nation's history. The government aren't going to give you the money for repairs, are they? Just imagine if someone broke in and stole these priceless little objects that Grandfather set so little store by that he didn't even insure them, or suppose the bad wiring sets off a fire and everything is destroyed, including poor old Mr and Mrs Barker. How would you feel then? Guilty of murder? It's not even as if you were stealing anything doing it my way."

"Isn't the bank going to be curious when it sees all these cheques going into Grandfather's account?"

"What cheques? This is strictly a cash transaction. That's how the purchasers like it, and that's how it's safest. You get a wad of notes that you can hide around the house, under floorboards, in hollow banisters, or wherever. Certainly some could go into Grandfather's account, as a big win from the horses, not that that's a likely story, but no one can prove otherwise, though it's probably safer in your mattress."

William flashed her a grin.

"Is that where yours is going?"

"Probably. It's not going into a bank for someone else to use, that's for sure. So, if you're agreeable, Granny, I'll phone Bloomy and tell him to pick me up tomorrow."

"Oh, by all means, Camilla, and I'm very grateful. It's a load off my mind. I've never been bothered by finances before, but Guy can't cope now, and I'm not sure I can."

Camilla went to the phone in the hall and dialled. Bloomy's mother answered.

"May I speak to Mr Bloomenthal, please," she asked in her best bred voice. "This is his assistant, Miss Bannerss."

Mrs Bloomenthal called loudly, "Benjy, telephone. It's your office."

Camilla smirked wickedly as he said hallo.

"Your mother said it was your office. I didn't know offices could talk, isn't that clever of it."

Bloomy could never tell if she was joking or sneering.

"Are you making fun of me?" he asked in a hurt voice.

"Most certainly not. You're much too clever to make fun of. I just want to tell you that it's on for tomorrow, all of it. I have the authority. We can take your American down with us if you think he can afford it. We'd better leave early, and take something to pack things with."

"Yes, I'll arrange all that. And believe me, he can afford it. American museums have bigger budgets than ours. We're going to be rich, Camilla," Bloomy said in a husky, unbelieving voice.

"I don't mind. I can live with that," she said and hung up.

"There is one other thing," Camilla said to the family when she came back. "In the downstairs lavatories there are some paintings, never noticed or declared because the valuers worked on the assumption that nothing worthwhile would be hung in a lavatory. Would you like us to find a private buyer for those?"

"What are they?" demanded William suspiciously. "I don't want my whole inheritance dissipated." Then, realising that this was not a very tactful remark under his Grandmother's present circumstances, he apologised. "Sorry Granny, but you know what I mean."

"The two in the gents are hideous Rowlandsons," Camilla said, quite unperturbed, "and there are two lovely pastel Marie Laurencins in the ladies. I suppose," she said to William, "you were terrified that I had found a hidden Canaletto, or was going to snatch some other great master from you."

William looked sheepishly guilty.

"They must have hung there a long time, won't they leave patches on the wall?" he asked.

"I'll buy some cheap and cheerful prints of the same size."

The heavy rumbling sound of the old lift put an end to further discussion.

"Here comes Guy," exclaimed Thea, jumping nervously to her feet. "I'll give you the letter you need after dinner, Camilla, and bless you."

Guy was wheeled in by his white-clad male nurse. He had suffered another small stroke which had left one hand rigid and the other permanently plucking at the rug which covered his knees.

"What's going on here?" he shouted as he came in. "Why is everybody standing around as if it was a wake? Why isn't anybody drinking?"

"We were waiting for you, Pa," Fifi said placatingly.

"Well, I'm here now, but we'll wait till he's gone," and he jerked his head towards the nurse. But too late, the nurse had already poured a splash of whisky into the glass, filled it with soda and presented it to Guy on a silver salver.

Guy snatched it, took a sip, made a face, and yelled.

"It's piss water! I want a real drink."

Quite unmoved the nurse said to Thea, "Ring if you need me," and left the room.

Guy started to cry.

"I'm dying. I know I'm dying. You know I'm dying. What difference can it make if I have a proper drink or not?"

Fifi, who had grown up in fear of her father, who knew him as a proud and domineering man, who had spent her adult life defying him, was overwhelmed with pity. She rushed over and put her arms round him as he sat weeping in his wheelchair.

"Oh, Pa, poor Pa," she exclaimed, and turned to Thea. "Surely it won't hurt him, one decent whisky?"

Thea hesitated, and then capitulated. William went to the decanter and poured a stiff whisky which he gave to his grandfather. Guy sucked it into his mouth, noisily and greedily, smacking his lips with pleasure. After a few minutes he perked up.

"You're getting too thin," he shouted at Fifi. "You should eat your porridge."

"Yuck," exclaimed Camilla.

"Not you," Guy said. "There's plenty of meat on you," and he put out a twitching hand and stroked her bottom which was clearly outlined in the tight jeans.

"Cut that out, you dirty old man!" Playfully she slapped his hand away. "I had enough trouble with you when I was young."

Guy chuckled happily, but Fifi, shocked, said tersely,

"You mustn't speak to your grandfather like that, Camilla," wondering what Camilla had meant by "trouble".

"Don't worry, Mumsy. I know how to deal with Grandfather, the old mauler. My school friends and I used to call him Lord Percy Filth because he couldn't keep his hands off us."

Guy chuckled and wheezed, not a bit abashed by these revelations.

"But you were just children!" cried Fifi, appalled.

"Little nymphs," exclaimed Guy, reaching out his hand for Camilla.

"He just wanted a little feel." Camilla skipped out of reach. "We used to tease him."

"Thea," Fifi appealed to her mother. "Why didn't you do something?"

Guy went into another paroxysm of wheezy laughter as Thea said defensively,

"I didn't know, did I? How could I know that he was so naughty?" and she patted his shoulder as if reproving a child.

The whisky did its work too well and Guy fell asleep in the middle of dinner. Thea had to ring and instruct the nurse to take her "dormouse" to bed.

18

Gazing out of the train window, Fifi watched the familiar countryside rush by with a feeling of nostalgia.

"You don't have to leave him, you don't have to leave him," said the wheels of the train in soporific rhythm.

She wished now that she had accepted Thea's offer to accompany her, to strengthen her resolve if she needed it. When Ron Matthew had told her that Ian – who had previously objected to all efforts on their part to speed up the financial and material details in advance of the divorce – had asked if she would go down to Bryony and decide what she wanted from the contents of the house, she had been jubilant. At last something was happening, being finally decided. She wouldn't feel she was living in limbo for much longer.

"Will Ian be there?" she asked nervously when the thought occurred to her. She had not seen Ian since his visit to Carol's flat, and felt hot with shame whenever she thought of it.

"I'm not sure. Would you like me to come with you?" Ron had offered sympathetically.

It seemed ridiculous to have your solicitor to chaperone you in case you met your husband, so Fifi had politely declined.

"Thank you, but I'll be all right. I don't know why I'm nervous. He isn't likely to be violent. Is he?"

Mentally she answered that question herself. Ian wouldn't be so undignified. She was the one who had lost control.

"I'm sure he won't. But if you change your mind and want me to come, you know where I am."

Carol had also offered to go with her, but Fifi had refused.

"I have to learn to cope on my own," she had said.

"Well, if he's there, don't let him get you into bed," warned Carol.

Fifi had laughed.

"After that last fiasco I don't imagine he'd want to. Ian isn't used to wild women."

Carol had given her a searching look.

"So, he had a surprise. He's probably excited by you for the first time in years, but you mustn't give in. If he gets you into bed your divorce goes out the window. You will have effectively condoned everything."

"There's no danger, either of Ian trying, or me succumbing, Fifi had assured her. "He may not be there anyway."

Now she was here, sitting in the train which always seemed to gather speed as it neared her station, nearing the house that had held so much happiness. My fool's paradise, Fifi thought bitterly.

Ian met her at the door, and paid for her taxi before she could stop him. She smiled to see that he was wearing the "children's uniform". Blue jeans and sneakers, and his strong brown arms were just the right contrast to the pale blue of the short-sleeved T-shirt. Fifi was surprised to see him in horn-rimmed glasses. He had worn glasses for reading before, but never with such heavy frames. They suited him and made her yearn for him more. Feeling awkward, she tried to make small talk, asking,

"Do you wear glasses all the time now, Ian?"

"Not all the time, no," he answered with a smile, "but I thought that, after our last encounter, it might be a sensible precaution – hoping, of course, that you fight Queensberry rules, and never strike a man wearing glasses."

Fifi burst out laughing.

"I'm sorry about that. It wasn't like me. I don't know what hit me."

"I know what hit me," he said ruefully, and rubbed the side of his head.

Then they were both laughing, the ice was broken. She felt completely at ease with him again.

"Would you like some coffee? I've just made it. Or do you

want to get started straight away? I had my secretary type out hundreds of 'his' and 'hers' labels."

"Coffee first would be nice."

"It's on the patio."

Why was I dreading this so much, Fifi wondered as she gazed out over the garden that she had planned and nursed, coaxed and nurtured for so many years.

"I miss the garden," she mused aloud.

"You don't have to," Ian answered, "It's here for you to come back to, to claim as your own, whenever you want it."

Fifi shook her head, surprised that she was not even tempted. In a way she still loved him but the chains of closeness had been broken and she felt lighter without them. She wanted to say to him, you were all I ever wanted and obviously never had, but she managed to say lightly,

"Remember me? I'm the one who never thought possessions were important, only people."

He put his hand over hers and patted it gently before leaving it resting there.

"You'd be surprised how much I remember about you, Fifi. How many times your values prevented me from being too destructive."

The comforting warmth of his hand on hers, and the kindness in his voice, brought tears to her eyes.

"We'd better get started," she said briskly, standing up. "We've got a lot to go through."

Ian put his arm around her, pressing his hand on her shoulder.

"A lifetime," he agreed.

They went through the downstairs rooms together, reminiscing, laughing over some memories, silently sad over others.

Ian had brought an assortment of Marks and Spencer's sandwiches down from London which they ate for lunch on the patio, washing them down with Fifi's favourite white wine. It was not Ian's favourite and, under normal circumstances, he would have had beer instead, but Fifi was touched to notice that he drank the wine without comment. They went upstairs afterwards and when he opened their bedroom door, she drew back. She remembered how many other afternoons they had come upstairs and made love, before sleeping the afternoon away. The memories crowded in.

Standing in the doorway, Ian turned her towards him, enclosing her with one arm and holding her head with the other hand as he always had. He pressed his lips to hers, slowly and gently sliding the tip of his tongue along the sensitive inner edge of her lower lip. She stiffened, responding immediately. Carol's warning rang in her head. Despairingly, Fifi forced her eyes open, thinking, this can't be happening. I mustn't let it happen. She tried to turn her head away and out of the corner of her eye caught the sight of her dressing table at a peculiar angle, and realised with a shock that at least two of the pictures Ian had taken had been taken here, in her bedroom, sitting at her dressing table. She pushed him forcefully away.

"Your body said yes," he said triumphantly.

"It was lying," she answered quickly. "I don't want anything from the bedroom anyway. Too many other women have used it."

Ian's surprise seemed genuine. Perhaps, she thought, he has forgotten the pictures, and the women in them. He shrugged.

"It would have been nice, Fifi, making love again in the afternoon with no interruptions, nothing to worry about. It was worth a try. I would give anything for another chance with you, Fifi, seriously. Think about it."

But Fifi had turned away to the linen cupboard and was saying uninterestedly,

"Shall we just split the linen down the middle, half and half?"

"Why not? That's what you've done to our marriage, Fifi."

"I have?" She glared at him and added, "And I've changed my mind. I would like something from the bedroom. I'd like the painting of the three children together."

"So would I," he stated bluntly. "You seem to have mustered the children to your side. They've demonstrated quite clearly where their loyalty lies. So, since you'll have the originals, I would like the picture."

"Oh, Ian. Don't try and tear the children apart and make them take sides. They love us both in different ways. You'll always be as much a part of them as I am. Only, just now, William and Camilla may feel I need extra support. You've always been so self sufficient."

"We won't argue about them," he said ungraciously. "I'll take the picture and have a copy made for you."

"That's par for the course," she murmured, smiling, "just like old times."

"What?"

"Never mind. Shall we do William's room?"

William's room was cold and airless.

"William said, if you don't mind, he'd like everything except the bed."

"How impractical of him. I should have thought the bed was the most important thing."

"He wants a double bed," Fifi explained.

Ian raised his eyebrows.

"Well, he is twenty-two," defended Fifi.

Without thinking, Ian hummed under his breath, "Following in father's footsteps, following his dear old Dad."

Fifi gasped.

"That's in very bad taste."

Ian stopped.

"Yes, I suppose it is. I'm sorry, Fifi. Today has been so like old times that I forgot. We used to have so many laughs together over things like that."

"In this case it isn't funny," declared Fifi, and burst into tears.

"Oh, Fifi! Why are you doing this to yourself?" Ian said uncomfortably. "We could still go on together. If I disgust you, we could have an arrangement like Guy and Thea. Together as a public couple and in private just companions, but separate. It's has worked well for them."

Fifi fumbled for a Kleenex and sniffed.

"Has it? You don't know how empty – and resentful – their lives were. I know, I had to live with it."

Ian said nothing, and they graduated to Percy's room.

"Percy doesn't want anything but his computer. He always leaves his clothes on the floor anyway, and he wants a bed that folds into the wall."

Ian laughed.

"He is the most peculiar chap. And what does little Camilla want from her bedroom?"

"Everything. She says she'll sort it out when it arrives. Maybe she's hoping to find some valuable antiques among her old toys."

"Will she live with you?"

"Good heavens, no. Camilla's very happy being landlady in her little flat. That way she can tell everybody what to do. I don't want to be told what to do any more."

"I was never overbearing," protested Ian indignantly.

At a quarter to six, Fifi decided it was time to leave.

"Do you mind if I phone for a taxi, Ian? I think I can make the 6.20."

"I'll drive you to the station," he offered.

Fifi accepted gratefully, then thought of all the locals who might see them at the station.

"That will cause a stir at the village pump, won't it?"

They smiled conspiratorially at each other. It had been one of the family sayings; any time anything untoward happened, someone would say it "would cause a stir at the village pump", though the village pump stood unused and isolated in the high street.

Ian stood and waited with her on the platform, amused at the covert stares they got.

Fifi found it embarrassing, trying to decide whether to nod to people she knew by sight, or pretend not to see them. Their separation was common knowledge so it was natural for people to be surprised to see them together. There would, no doubt, be a lot of whispers of a reconciliation hissed about the village. Ian was thinking the same thing, and was pleased. As the train pulled out of the station he said to himself, you'll come back to me, Fifi. You're a woman of habit. You've made me your life, and you won't be happy living alone. And, filled with self satisfaction, he imagined the party he would give when all this nonsense had subsided.

Watching his figure diminish as the train gathered speed, Fifi felt as if a dark cloud had suddenly been lifted. There was relief that she could sit in silence, alone, for the rest of the journey. She thought of the garden, of the back-breaking hours she had had to spend to keep it in perfect order. She remembered how she and Gladys had dusted and polished, scrubbed and ironed, so that the house would be perfect for Ian and his friends at the weekends. It seemed to her incredible now that it had all seemed so important.

Carol was out when she finally got back to the flat. With joy, she slammed the front door, kicked off her shoes, threw herself flat on the floor and yelled to the empty room,

"Free at last!"

19

When you are not quite sure where you want to live, and are in no hurry, and don't even know how much you will be able to spend on a flat, flat hunting can be quite a time-consuming, though entertaining, business, Fifi decided as she roamed as far as Highgate Village in her search.

Thea had offered her the old mews cottage over the garage, that had once housed the family chauffeur. When that was refused as too small for Percy's wall bed, Thea suggested that she have a suite of rooms in the main house. Camilla vetoed this, saying that Fifi would be exchanging one cage for another. She insisted that Fifi needed a place of her own so that she could be independent, like Greatgranny. Percy had agreed, and William had just said cautiously that it was up to Fifi herself to decide.

As it happened, Fifi would probably have gone on living with Carol, paying her share and enjoying Carol's company when she wanted it. They got on very well together, allowing each other privacy and independence, but Carol's first ex-husband had moved in for a couple of weeks and, since there were only two bedrooms, he was in with Carol. He had been there overnight before Fifi found out and she immediately offered to move out and stay at Thea's, but Carol had replied,

"Don't be silly. I don't mind him sleeping with me, we were married, and he is Jason's father, so it isn't immoral. It's only for a few days anyway. He had hoped to stay with Jason, until he discovered that Jason was in a squat, so he came here. I couldn't turn him away, it was very late, and a little uncomplicated sex is quite nice once in a while."

"Yes," Fifi had agreed. "It would be. Sex is the problem I can't find the answer to. What do healthy women like me, who've always had an active sex life, do when it suddenly stops?

The thought of casual sex appalls me, and I never want to get emotionally involved again, but I still need it. Is there an answer?"

"I shouldn't think so, not with the specification you mention – unless you buy a vibrator," Carol had replied with a laugh.

"Forget it," said Fifi. "It's not that I'm a prude, but it's so cold-blooded."

As the days had passed, Fifi noticed that Ted and Carol were becoming inseparable, and she wondered if the arrangement was going to become permanent. She didn't dislike Ted, there was nothing to dislike, but she felt that a threesome on a permanent basis would be uncomfortable, and lead to friction, so she tactfully began to look for a place of her own. The day Ted left to return to the Isle of Man, Carol came into Fifi's bedroom. She sat down on the bed and refilled her mug from Fifi's coffee pot.

"Ted's asked me to marry him again," she announced.

"Are you pleased?" Fifi asked cautiously.

"Not particularly. I thought I would feel triumphant, but I don't. I know what it is. He's getting too old to chase women, and he's lonely. He wants to settle down now."

"And have you hand him his slippers?"

"Exactly. And have someone with shared memories so he can play the old 'do you remember when?', 'do you remember who?' game. Conversation without effort."

"And?"

"And I said no. I may live to regret it, but I doubt it. I've been my own boss too long. I'm the one who chooses which TV channel to watch, when I eat, when I go to bed and get up. I couldn't do the waiting around, the tidying up bit, any more. I'm not lonely, and I've grown too comfortable and selfish. I like my own place, with things where I put them. Giving all that up is too high a price to pay for a roll in the hay. Oh, I made a poem, call me Shakespeare."

"I call you smart. I'm glad you've decided as you have. I wouldn't have felt right if you had remarried Ted just because I was sleeping in your spare room. Lust doesn't last forever, as well I know. Now you'll have time to come flat hunting with me."

"You don't need a flat," protested Carol. "You're welcome in this one."

"I know, but hunting is fun, and you meet the nicest people."

When Violet heard that Fifi was looking for a place of her own, she invited her down to the cottage to choose any "bits and pieces" she might fancy for herself.

Violet followed, as Fifi browsed round the cottage, suggesting various items.

"I'm leaving the cottage to Camilla," Violet said, "so you had better take anything you want now."

Fifi glanced at her suspiciously.

"You're not feeling ill, are you?"

She wondered if this was her grandmother's tactful way of telling her something she knew she wouldn't want to hear.

"No, but I'm old, and death is to be expected by the elderly."

"Don't expect it yet," pleaded Fifi. "I haven't seen enough of you recently."

"My dear Fifi, time doesn't stand still. We all have to bow to the inevitable. The orientals are so much wiser than we are about death. Now find something pretty to take your mind off the subject."

Fifi chose carefully. A set of Victorian paintings, a Chippendale tripod table, a Queen Anne grandfather clock and two Shaker chairs that Violet always kept hanging from pegs on the wall. The Shakers had made all their simple furniture to hang on the walls when not in use so that they would not be in the way for the second coming of the Lord. Fifi had a much less pious thought; in a small flat they would be there for visitors, and out of the way for family. She also took two silver tankards of the Queen Anne period, and the old Georgian silver that had been in Violet's family for generations.

Fifi had been driven down in Thea's car and Violet beamed approval as the chauffeur put Fifi's collection in the back.

"Minimum quantity – maximum quality," she applauded. "You still have an eye for real value, Fifi."

"I only hope I haven't chosen things that Camilla had her heart set on."

Violet cackled happily.

"Neither you nor Ian know that daughter of yours. If Camilla sees something she wants, she takes it. Her room at the Boltons must look like Aladdin's Cave."

"But she doesn't live at the Boltons any more," Fifi explained.

"I know, but she keeps all her treasures there. I've given her a lot. She tells me that they're safe there from prying eyes and sticky fingers. Oh, that little girl does make me laugh. So don't worry about Camilla, she'll always get what she wants."

At that very moment, Camilla was wondering how she was going to get what she wanted, which was to be included in the group that was going to Montreal to catalogue and value a hitherto unknown collection. Bloomy was going, as was Anthony Gilbert for the paintings. But four tickets had been booked, and no announcement made as to who the other two would be. It might be Harvey, if there were books, or Davis, for sculpture, but Camilla was only a trainee and what hope did she have? This was her day to lunch with Bloomy, how could she broach the subject?

They met at La Recolte, where they were not likely to be seen by anyone from the office, though Bloomy's lust had long since dispatched his desire for caution. It was only Camilla who insisted. Now he had his commission from the sale of the Earl of Cheswick's netsuke, he felt he could afford to offer her the trip to Montreal, and pay for it out of his own money. No one could deny that she was an excellent secretary.

Over the avocados he said, "I would like to take you to Montreal, Camilla, would you come?"

He had said "I" so she knew it was not a company offer. She recognised it for what it was, and was considering how best to accept it without unseemly alacrity when Bloomy, frightened that she was trying to word a refusal, added, lyingly, "No strings attached."

Camilla gave him her most beautiful smile. She knew what a coward he was where she was concerned.

"Alright then, thank you, Bloomy. Separate rooms are best, but I don't object to unlocked communicating doors. We just don't want to get talked about in the office."

Bloomy's heart swelled with gratitude.

"You won't regret it," he promised.

I'll make sure I don't, Camilla promised herself. After this he would want to take her everywhere with him. She would meet all the great continental experts, listen and learn, and in a few years she would be accepted by them for herself and her talents, not just as Bloomy's assistant. In the meantime, she would be indispensable.

20

Ian was not a man to accept defeat. He knew all the tricks of evasion and procrastination. He was sure that the longer he delayed the financial settlement for the divorce, the more time Fifi would have to reconsider the inadvisability of it. When her solicitor, Ron Matthews, produced a figure suitable for her settlement, Ian would manage to be unavailable to peruse it for weeks at a time. Then he would question everything, argue everything, and finally have Mr Cross, his own solicitor, produce another, completely ludicrous figure. Neither had Ian put Bryony on the market, though he knew that, eventually, Fifi was entitled to half the proceeds. He was generous when it came to paying her a monthly allowance, but a lump sum meant he had accepted severance and that he would not do. He intended to keep her dependent on him as long as he could.

July arrived and Fifi was preparing to take William, Camilla and Percy to the Algarve. She contacted Ron Matthew to say she would be away and he asked her to come in and see him. She went, full of hope that he would have the final papers for her to sign. Ron explained the situation to her.

"I think we've now got to call his bluff. Does he have your address in Portugal?"

"No." Fifi could be sure of that. She had not, as yet, given it to anyone.

"Good. Then the day you leave I will contact Mr Cross and tell him that, due to the length of time Mr Bannerss is taking to deal with this matter, my client has decided to go to court on the original count of infidelity, and to ask the court to order provision for her and her younger son. In which case there will be no further need for any communications between the parties concerned until the date set. Are you prepared to go with that?"

"Yes, I suppose I am. We don't seem to have any alternative, do we?"

"No, we don't. Your husband is a very pig-headed man and used to having his own way, but I'm no longer prepared to be a yo-yo on his string. If the settlement we've already asked for is immediately forthcoming after my communication, then I will accept it. Anything else they try to use to cause further delay, I shall return it with the information that the matter is no longer negotiable."

Fifi agreed and gave him her address and telephone number in Vale de Lobo, in case of emergency.

On Thursday, she and Percy, and Percy's friend Gerald, flew to Faro. William and his girlfriend, Anna, flew down the following day, and Camilla, who had managed to get an extra four weeks unpaid holiday out of Bloomy, arrived on the Saturday with her flatmate, Daphne.

Thea had intended to accompany them when the holiday was first mooted, but felt that now she dare not leave Guy even a day, let alone one month, so Carol decided to join Fifi at the end of the first week.

It was an idyllic place to spend a holiday. The villa, with its large cool rooms, and great stone terrace, was on a hill overlooking the golf course. Steps from the terrace led down to the blue, circular swimming pool, with its barbecue area. They were in easy walking distance of the beach, the small cluster of shops, the restaurants and disco, and the tennis courts. Fifi had hired two cars, but they were seldom used. She took one to go to the supermarket twice a week, but all the excursions they planned were put off to "tomorrow" as the weather was too good to waste sightseeing. Fifi had never had a holiday before where so little was expected of her. Everyone got their own breakfast at different times, and piled their plates into the dishwasher. The maid came and made the beds and washed the floors. Sometimes Fifi invited them all to lunch at a little beach restaurant where they overindulged in the wonderful local wine, and had to sleep for an afternoon; otherwise everyone made a snack for lunch and Fifi prepared dinner, a meal they all ate together. If it was a barbecue, Percy and Gerald cooked it and whatever it was, they always ate outside, under the stars. Afterwards they might wander down to the square for a drink or a coffee. Camilla and Daphne often went to the disco, William and Anna walked hand in hand along the beach, and Fifi preferred not to know what Percy and Gerald were up to. Some nights they swam, or watched a video on the machine in the villa.

Everybody was relaxed and happy. There were no squabbles, fights or complaints. Fifi regained all the weight she had lost and put on a bit more. She was tanned and healthy looking, all signs of strain gone.

Floating on the pool on a lilo one morning she said dreamily to Carol, "This is the best holiday I've ever had. In fact, it's the first holiday I've ever had. When we went away before we always went somewhere where Ian knew someone else had taken a villa, so that he had a partner for golf and tennis. And, of course, he wanted to entertain them. We had luncheon guests, and dinner guests, or we'd have to go out, and that meant arranging something for the children to eat before I went. It was always a rush and a hassle and a lot of work. I was usually glad to get home. But now, I'm in heaven. Do you know, I don't think I've had shoes on since I arrived."

"I know just what you mean," agreed Carol, stirring the ice in her white port with her finger. "Unfortunately men expect you to enjoy what they enjoy, whether it's football or their friends. And they think meals prepare and cook themselves."

"I do hope William isn't going to be like that."

"It will be someone else's problem if he is."

"But I shall feel guilty," protested Fifi.

"Do you think Ian's mother feels guilty?"

"She's dead, so I don't know. I never met her. It's hard to imagine Ian having a mother." The idea made Fifi laugh so hard she fell off the lilo.

"There's no more vino verdi for you on an empty stomach," called Percy in an imitation of Ian's voice as Fifi rose spluttering to the surface. "Is this a good moment to tell you I'm not going back to school?"

Fifi was stunned.

"Have you been expelled?"

"No, I just decided to leave."

"Percy!" Fifi heaved herself out of the pool. "Your father will be very disappointed if you don't stay on for the sixth form."

"No, he won't. I wrote to him before the term ended. He wrote back saying 'If you're not returning to school you'd better decide what you will be doing because after school comes work'."

"Didn't he ask you why?"

"Not exactly."

"What does that mean, Percy?"

Percy glanced at Gerald who was snorkelling along the surface of the swimming pool, then dropped his voice.

"He said he realised that the separation was turning my world upside down, and that it was an even greater shock to me than it had been to him. He had known it would ruin my school work, and lose me friends, but he didn't want me to lose the chance of a fine education because . . ." Percy stopped, and looked miserable.

"Because what?" asked Fifi gently.

"Because you were prepared to ruin everyone else's life to satisfy a menopausal whim."

"My God!" Carol was on her feet. "That fornicating bastard! If you don't tell Percy what it's all about, I will!"

"I already know what it's all about," Percy said. "William told me. I think it's perfectly disgusting, an old man like Dad. I worked especially hard for good passes to prove him wrong, but I think I've failed everything. I want to leave Eton because I don't want to use any of his money, ever again," and he turned and hurried, shoulders hunched, into the villa.

Fifi was too shocked to speak. Gerald drifted by her, took the tube from his mouth, and said, "I shouldn't worry, Lady F. I expect he's passed all his subjects. He's just lost his cool at the moment." Then he put the tube back in his mouth and slithered away.

Later, Fifi told Camilla what had been said. Camilla told William, William told everybody else that there was to be a family confab that evening to discuss Percy's future with him. They sat around roasting bananas on the barbecue, whilst Percy informed them of a job he'd been offered.

"Just up my street," he announced proudly. "Woodley's father said he'd take me on and train me. He's a bookmaker."

"There's a lot of money to be made there," Carol applauded his choice.

"You're under age, I think." Fifi hoped she was right. She couldn't remember if it was in pubs or bookmakers that you had to be over eighteen. She hoped it was bookmakers because she wanted Percy to finish his education before he decided on a career anyway.

"As far as I'm concerned it would be worthwhile you leaving just to see Dad's face when he has to say, 'my son the bookie', instead of 'my son at Eton'."

This sally caused Camilla and Daphne to laugh so much they cried.

"Did you keep the letter?" Fifi asked casually.

"Yes, it's with my stuff at Granny's."

"I think my solicitor would like to see it," Fifi said, adding, "I can pay your school fees myself. In fact, I shall insist on doing so if you decide to go back. Of course, you could always go to a sixth form college in London."

"As a day boy, you mean?"

"Yes, I'd be very happy with that."

"So would I," said Percy.

"Lucky sod!" muttered Gerald.

Camilla wandered into the kitchen the next evening and offered to help prepare dinner.

"Shall I wash the salad?" she suggested.

"You have to put those purifying tablets in the water and leave the lettuce to soak for ten minutes."

"Whatever for?"

"In case the germs in the water get on the salad."

"I should think we Brits are immune to any germs in the water considering what we have to drink at home." She splashed the lettuce up and down. "You've got to do something about Dad, you know. He only appreciates the sort of people who kick his teeth in, which is what I feel like doing now."

"Yes, so do I. My solicitor has told him that we won't wait any longer for him to decide on a financial settlement. We're going to court without it and we're going to ask the judge to make the decision. It may mean that I shall have to name co-respondents, so there will be a lot of irate husbands after your father."

"Good."

"I didn't want to have a scandal because of you children, but," Fifi stopped speaking and held hard to the back of the chair, stricken. "I would never have believed your father could be so vindictive as to try and turn Percy against me. I've never tried to hurt him. And whats the point of his pretending that he wants me back, that he's against the divorce?"

"He's against the divorce because it wasn't his idea, and it ruins the image he had of himself. His effort with Percy backfired anyway. The trouble with you, Mumsy, is that you're too innocent. You don't recognise a grade A shit when you see one. Never mind, you have all of us to look after you."

"But that's the wrong way round. I should be looking after you."

"You did that when we needed it most; now it's our turn."

The thought of what Ian might have said in other letters, and to other people, put a blight on that day and the next for Fifi, but eventually she managed to put it out of her mind and the long, lazy, sunny days wove their magic again.

On the Monday, three days before Fifi was due to go home, the telephone rang.

"That'll be Ron Matthews," she cried, sensing victory at last. "It's to tell me that Ian has finally capitulated."

126

But it was Thea to tell Fifi that Guy had died in his sleep that morning. Thea wanted them all to come home immediately. The perfect holiday, like the perfect marriage, had ended imperfectly, thought Fifi sadly, as she began packing.

Getting back to England was not as easy as they had expected. They had eight seats reserved for the Thursday flight and, as it was high season, everything seemed fully booked. Fifi managed to get William and Anna to Paris, and thence to London, on the day Thea had telephoned. As William was the heir, Fifi expected he would be more help to Thea, and therefore should go first. Camilla and Percy had to fly at 8 a.m. the next morning to Lisbon, and then to Heathrow, and Fifi herself, with Daphne, Gerald and Carol, had to fly to Gatwick on the Wednesday. Thea sent the car down to fetch them.

The first thing that struck Fifi as she walked into the house was the feeling of brightness. It seemed full of light and air, as if all the windows and doors had been opened. Even the ceilings seemed higher. She entered the study without the usual feeling of dread that she had felt all her adult life. She thought of Pa, the way he filled any room he was in, his noisiness, his sarcasm, his supreme egoism. She had been afraid of him as a child, and hid the fear behind defiance as an adult. Now he was gone, as if a huge black cloud had blown away. She buried her face in her hands and wept with relief.

Finding her thus, Thea mistook her tears for grief.

"Don't cry, darling," she comforted. "He was quite paralysed the last two days so it was a release."

Fifi took a handkerchief from her bag and blew her nose. It would be useless to try and explain to Thea her feelings for Pa. The longing for his love, the occasional sign of approval, the almost constant rejection.

"Yes, I know," she agreed. "It is much better this way."

"He's left you a very rich woman, Fifi."

"Me? But, but ..." Fifi stuttered in her astonishment. "What about you? What about William?"

Thea smiled.

"I told you once before that I would be all right. The house is mine, and I shall eventually leave it to Percy. Guy left me an income for life, the capital of which reverts to William on my death. William will get everything that is entailed in the estate which, thanks to Camilla's astute dealings, will be in good repair. The manor is covered in tarpaulins, planks and workmen at the moment, but that's temporary, and I gather from William that he has some excellent plans for the future. But you, you were the surprise. You have inherited an enormous trust fund started by Guy when you were born. Knowing his own terrible propensity for gambling he had it drawn up so that even he couldn't touch it. There was one codicil though; if you had a brother at any date, then everything would revert to the son. The trust matured when you were twenty-one, but he'd either forgotten it, or decided to let it accumulate. He probably wanted to make sure that Ian provided for you. Guy believed in the old values, that a man should provide for his wife."

"I just can't believe it," said Fifi, shaking her head.

"He did love you in his way, Fifi. I know he wasn't very demonstrative, but he thought public affection was bad form. Women were for sex, men for friendship, and children for the continuance of the line. Perhaps the money will serve to remind you how much he appreciated you for continuing the line for him. Each time you had a baby he would say to Barker, 'Notch one up, Barker, that's another LeRoser,' and Barker would take six bottles of champagne downstairs."

Fifi put her hand over Thea's.

"You know if you ever want anything, whatever I have is yours for the asking."

"I'll keep the offer in reserve," said Thea. "By the way, Granny isn't coming to the funeral. She says the next funeral she has to sit through will be her own."

Fifi laughed.

"It must be wonderful to be able to say exactly what you feel."

"But not always diplomatic! Ian's telephoned a few times.

I didn't speak to him myself. He asked William about funeral arrangements, and what he could do, etcetera. He even offered to put mourners up at Bryony, if you can imagine such impertinence. William said, very coldly, that we were waiting for your return to finalise everything, but that he thought you would find the idea of your own relations as guests in the house that had once belonged to you, with your ex-husband as host, indelicate to say the least. I've no doubt he was angling for an invitation to the chief mourners' car."

"No, thank you," Fifi said determinedly.

"That's what I thought," Thea said. "Now you have to help get me some suitable black garments."

21

The church was packed. Not only had the whole village turned out to pay their respects, but nephews and nieces with their respective families, distant cousins, tenant farmers and staff, were all there.

Fifi sat beside Thea in the front pew, with William, Camilla and Percy along the row. Above the hushed murmur of voices, Fifi distinctly heard William hiss, "Spread out, and duck your heads."

She frowned and turned to glare at him, but found all three had moved apart, and were sitting with their heads in their hands as if in prayer. Fifi found it hard to relate this pious action to William's sibilant command. Then she heard Ian's familiar footsteps approaching. They stopped within feet of her and she also quickly closed her eyes. This was not the time or the place for them to meet.

He stood there for what seemed like ages, hoping one of the children would raise their heads so that he could attract their attention. He had not expected there to be such a large congregation, and in spite of the extra chairs put in the aisles there were no seats left, except those in the front pew for the immediate family. Fifi put her hand over her eyes, and waited. Her children also waited, holding their breath. After a few minutes, Fifi heard Ian walk angrily away.

With his jaw set, and his eyes cold, he went and stood at the back of the church. He was livid with rage. He felt humiliated, publicly repudiated. He had always sat in the family pew. He stared hard at the back of Fifi's head, willing her to turn and beckon him. He noticed that her hair had grown again, but instead of wearing it loose as he liked, she had it drawn back and tied at the nape of her neck with a soft black bow. She was simply and smartly dressed in mourning black. She looked tanned and well. Soft and relaxed, he thought longingly, feeling a sudden desire for her.

As the hymns filled the church, Ian knew that he was becoming as obsessed with her as he had been before they were married. He saw William go to the lectern and felt a momentary glow of pride. That was *his* wife. That was *his* son. They were all *his* children. And they were sitting with *his* wife. He felt depressed, shut out.

Near the end of the service, the Vicar beckoned to William, who walked calmly to the lectern and took out a piece of paper.

Fifi's throat went dry as it always did when one of them was asked to perform, whether in a football match or on the piano. She had not known that William would be expected to speak, but obviously it was something he had arranged with the vicar, who had baptised and confirmed each member of the family in turn. Knowing that both William and Percy were very upset by Guy's death, it occurred to her that William might become emotional, and break down – in public! She squirmed with embarrassment at the thought, and then reprimanded herself mentally. You're getting as bad as Pa, she thought. What does it matter if he does cry, people do. It doesn't matter.

But William stood, gazing out over the congregation with his startled blue eyes, looking very young in spite of his beard, and read with great self possession:

> "Death is only an old door
> set in a garden wall,
> On gentle hinges it gives, at dusk
> when the thrushes call.
> Along the lintel are green leaves,
> Beyond the light lies still"
> Very willing and weary feet
> Go over that sill.

131

There is nothing to trouble any heart;
Nothing to hurt at all.
Death is only a quiet door
in an old wall."

Then he came back to the pew and sat down. Fifi smiled proudly at him. Now she could relax . . . but not for long. The Vicar was beckoning to Percy. Percy, who had wept unashamedly in his grandfather's bedroom. This was too much of an ordeal for him, Fifi decided, and put out her hand to signal to him that he need not go, but he smiled his old mischievous smile at her and whispered, "I won't say anything about the Four Horses of the Apocalypse, or the other horses!"

Even more self-assured than William, he took his place at the lectern. He needed no paper, but spoke from memory.

"For what is it to die but to stand naked in the wind and to melt into the sun? And what is it to cease breathing but to free the breath from its restless tides, that it may rise and expand and seek God unencumbered?"

Then he too returned and sat down.

Having worried about William and Percy having to speak, Fifi now worried that Camilla would feel rejected and ignored, because she had not had an opportunity.

"Would you like to say something, Camilla?" she whispered. Camilla pulled a face.

"Only if I get paid for it," she whispered back. "This is one of the Vicar's experiments. He thinks it's a good idea to involve the young in a family death. He says he thinks they'll be able to accept it more easily, but death is death anyway, and you have to accept it."

"How very wise of you, Camilla, dear," said Thea, biting back a smile.

After the blessing had been said and the bearers came for the coffin, the Vicar addressed the congregation.

"Only the immediate family will be coming to the graveside, so I would be grateful if the congregation remain seated until the mourners have left by the side door. Then you may all leave by the main door."

Ian turned to leave by the main door at once – no one could stop him going to the graveside once he was outside – but he found himself face to face with Brian and Janice.

Brian gave him a shamefaced grin.

"We were late here too. I can tell you it was a relief to see you standing as well. Are you coming up to the Manor for the 'do'?"

Furious that Brian had noticed the snub he had received by being excluded, both from the family pew and the graveside, as if twenty-three years of a relationship could be wiped out in seconds, Ian tried to salvage some of his dignity.

"Of course I am," he said with well-simulated surprise. "It's my son's home now."

As soon as Ian's car entered the great wrought-iron gates, passed the gatehouse and took its place in the slow-moving queue of cars crawling up the three miles of tree-lined drive that led to the Manor, he was able to see the enormous renovations that were taking place. An army of landscape gardeners were working on the flower beds, the maze and the fountains. What looked like a dredger was down by the artificial lake. Scaffolding covered one whole wing of the house, and although the workmen had been dismissed for the afternoon, evidence of their work was everywhere. Where had Guy got the money? Had he had a premonition of his own death and decided to prepare the place for William? With a jolt, Ian realised that William would be living here, in this splendour which made Bryony look like a gardener's cottage. Would Fifi live here with him? It would ruin Ian's plans if she had that choice.

He had tried to browbeat her, and had failed. She had turned on him physically. He had tried to win her back with the charm that had successfully brought him almost any woman he had wanted, and that too had failed, though, for a minute or two when she was back at Bryony with him, he had thought he had succeeded. He had been willing to play a waiting game, but then he had received the ultimatum from her solicitor. He knew he could not risk her naming names. It would make him too many enemies. He had had to agree to the settlement demanded, but he'd make her wait for it. Beg for it. He had decided to stall over selling the house. That would be feasible considering the state of the property market. She wouldn't be able to buy a place to live in until he gave her a lump sum. He would keep her short of money for as long as was possible, until she regretted her hasty action. Then they would renew their vows in the local church again, and it would be a fresh start. He did not want any other woman now, he just wanted Fifi. Ian had been nursing this plan for a month, and Guy's death might ruin it if Fifi came here to live with William.

His thoughts churned on even as he parked his car. He had understood that the estate was short of money, but expensive caterers had taken over inside, and from the look of the work outside, it was a case of rumour running away with truth.

Once inside, Ian found few people that he knew. Mutual acquaintances treated him with studied politeness. They were obviously embarrassed by his presence. He didn't belong any more and everyone knew it, and were wondering why he didn't know it. This was Fifi's world of grace and breeding. His was the world of business and money.

Brian brought over two clients of his and introduced them to Ian.

"Gerring and Berry are in estate management and development, so if William wants any help with his project they're more than willing to pick up a piece of the action," he said hopefully.

Ian had not had a chance to talk to William, and had no idea what his project was, but he also had no intention of admitting his ignorance.

"I'll mention it to him," he said easily, "but this is not the occasion. Excuse me, I must find Fifi."

He found Camilla instead.

"Where's your mother?" he asked.

"Indulging in a menopausal whim, I expect," Camilla said sarcastically.

"What?" Ian looked distinctly puzzled.

"As you said in your letter to Percy."

"Oh, I see. That was written at a very low moment when I was hurt by your mother's attitude towards me," he defended himself, "and since he wants to drop out of school I was right in thinking that it has affected him adversely. And I do think his school work this last term will have suffered as a result."

"Well, it hasn't. We got his results. He got five A's, four B's and two C's, and you can't do better than that" she announced triumphantly.

Ian was nonplussed, but said weakly, "Well, that's excellent news. I must congratulate him. He'll certainly have to stay on at Eton for his A levels now."

"Actually, he's going to a sixth form college in London from now on, and," Camilla added, "William got honours."

"Did he? A successful family indeed. By the way, what is this project of William's?"

"You mean the Orangerie?"

"If that's what it is, yes."

"He's going to open the gardens, and some of the house during the summer, and turn the Orangerie into a caff. He's going to call it 'The Great British Breakfast', and that's all that will be served. A plate of sausages, bacon, eggs, tomato, mushrooms and fried bread. Tea, toast and marmalade. £6 all in. I expect it will be a roaring success."

"So do I," agreed Ian. "But it'll need financing." He was thinking he wouldn't mind investing in a venture like that, but Camilla said,

"He's got all that arranged already," and she sped off to talk to other guests.

Ian continued his search for Fifi, and finally found her in the small music room where Thea had collected all Guy's family together.

"Hello, Fifi, my dear," he greeted her. "I am so sorry. This has not been a very propitious year for you."

"No," she agreed coldly.

135

"It seemed so strange being in our church today and not sitting with you. It brought back so many memories for me, as I expect it did for you."

"I was burying my father, not taking a trip down memory lane," she answered tartly. "Just what is it you want of me, Ian? Because I am getting very tired of having you on the periphery of my life, hovering."

She was as surprised at her tone of voice as Ian was. She was thinking in amazement that this was the first time that she had seen him without her heart leaping for joy. She felt neither anger nor desire nor regret. I don't seem to be feeling anything at all, she thought, apart from a minor prickle of annoyance that he's here.

Ian lowered his voice, hoping not to be overheard.

"You know what I want of you, Fifi. I want a chance to rebuild our marriage, to . . ."

Fifi held up her hand to stop him saying anything further.

"No. Forget it. You asked me if today brought back any memories. It brought back one. Vows. Vows that you constantly broke. There is no marriage to rebuild. I understand from Mr Matthews that we are due in court soon, and . . ."

"We have to talk about that, Fifi." he interrupted her.

"No talk. No negotiations. It's all over. I don't want to be married to anyone, and especially not to you. I am very happy as I am. Life has given me a second chance, a chance to be on my own, to start again, and I'm taking it." And she turned her back on him and walked away.